HALLOWEEN
TALES

HALLOWEEN TALES

Edited by

Kate Jonez

Omnium Gatherum
Los Angeles CA

Halloween Tales
Edited by Kate Jonez

Anthology Copyright © 2014
Individual stories copyright by individual authors.

"Dead Devil in the Freezer" first appeared in *Cemetery Dance* in a slightly edited form. Copyright 2001 by Nancy Holder.

"The Devil Came to Mamie's on Hallowe'en" by Lisa Morton originally appeared in *Cemetery Dance* #60.

"The Hairy Ones" by Terry M. West is part of the collection *What Price Gory?* released in 2013 through Pleasant Storm Entertainment, Inc.

"Outlaws of Hill Country" by John Palisano first appeared in *Harvest Hill*, from Graveside Tales, 2009.

"Ankou, King of the Dead" was first published in *Doorways Magazine*, Issue 7, October, 2008.

"Johnny Jackson's School Dare" previously published in a collection.

ISBN-13: 978-0692261033
ISBN-10: 0692261036

First Edition

TABLE OF CONTENTS

"Where there is no imagination there is no horror."

—Sir Arthur Conan Doyle

"...the simple country folk came to believe that on October 31st the fairies forsook their hiding-places to dance in the forest glades, while witches, goblins, and other evil spirits held revels in deserted abbeys, or plotted against mankind in the shadows of ruinous castles and keeps."

—Martha Russell Orne,
Halloween: How to Celebrate It
(1898—the first book on Halloween)

THE DEVIL CAME TO MAMIE'S ON HALLOWE'EN

By Lisa Morton

It was Hallowe'en night, and business was slow at the whorehouse.

Leona didn't put much stock in the stories that kept other folk indoors on this night. She'd laughed over stories about Jacky-Ma-Lantern, who'd once outsmarted the Bad Man and then couldn't get into Hell or Heaven, and so on Hallowe'en he wandered around lighting his way with a coal kept in a pumpkin. She'd once seen the strange blue lights in the bayou that some said led unwary travelers to their doom on this night, but she didn't really believe they were spirits. And her favorite of Miss Mamie's girls, Lizzie, had talked about going down to New Orleans once and meeting up with a real hoodoo man, who she'd watched bring a dead boy back to life on All Saints' Day. But as much as Leona loved Lizzie, she thought even decent, smart folk could sometimes be bamboozled when they found something they just plain *wanted* to believe in.

It was about midnight now ("the witching hour", Leona remembered Lizzie once calling it), and the swamp just behind Miss Mamie's was dark and quiet, no flatboats poling up to the dock tonight, unloading new customers. Leona wondered again where Lizzie had gotten to; Beulah, the cook, said she'd left out the back door about four that afternoon, just as the sun was going down. She'd taken a big kettle with her, and said she'd be back around night. It wasn't safe to wander around the bayou *any* night, and Leona couldn't imagine where Lizzie had gone.

It didn't help that Mamie's scrawny old cat, Lumpy (so named because he was as black as a lump of coal), was missing, too.

So Leona sat on the back porch, waiting, hoping one or the other would show up soon. Beulah had already gone home, and the kitchen was cool but the night was unseasonably warm and humid. Usually she'd have to be in the main parlor, playing the piano for the customers, but there weren't many of them tonight.

Leona cranked the phonograph again, and settled back on the old splintered wood of the porch steps to listen to Ma Rainey. Harold, Miss Mamie's bartender and muscle, had been into town today, and Leona had given him seventy-five cents to get the record for her. It was "Traveling Blues", and Leona swayed back and forth, humming along, as the song spilled out of the phonograph's big horn.

I went to the depot, looked up and down the board,
I went to the depot, looked up and down the board,
I asked the ticket agent, "It's my time on this road?"

Leona had listened to the song enough now that she'd be able to play it on the piano when she went back in; if anyone wanted to hear, she could sing it, too.

Fact was, she thought she could sing it just as good as Ma Rainey herself.

One of the funny things about Miss Mamie was that she only wanted live music at her "establishment"; she claimed the menfolk didn't want to hear just records, although Leona knew plenty of menfolk who liked Bessie Smith and Ma Rainey and Sippie Wallace. Miss Mamie, though, said she'd paid plenty of money for that piano, and live music gave her place "a touch of class." Truthfully, Leona was glad, because it gave her a way to make herself useful around Mamie's place—she had a natural gift for the piano and for singing.

Unfortunately, even those gifts wouldn't carry her much longer.

Miss Mamie had come into the kitchen yesterday afternoon, before most of the other women had even gotten up yet, and she'd called Leona away from the washing and sat her down at the table. Mamie'd just gotten back from doing some banking in town, and she was dressed up, looking fine for a woman of forty. It was no wonder she still got customers requesting her services.

"That Jackson Smith done asked about you again last night," she'd said, while lighting a cigarette.

Leona had tried not to squirm. "That so?"

"Um-hmm." Miss Mamie took a drag from her smoke, then went on. "He'd pay extra for you, Leona, since it'd be your first time. We'd both make some mighty nice money off'n it."

"I'm not doin' nothin' with Jackson Smith," Leona had replied.

"He's not so bad," Mamie said, squinting at Leona through her tobacco haze.

"I know he's not, Miss Mamie, but I..."

At that point Mamie had actually set the cigarette down and leaned across the table, and Leona'd had to struggle not to lean back, away. "Now you listen to me, child: You sixteen years old, you a woman now. I promised your mama, God bless her, to look after you 'til you was growed. She was one of the finest ladies I ever had work for me, and I owed her, but I figure the time you growed is *now*. I can't keep carryin' you, Leona—"

Leona had cut her off. "But Miss Mamie, you your own self said I was the best piano player you's ever likely to hear—"

"I did, but, honey, we need somebody to play something livelier here, not those slow things you like. You put a few drinks in these boys and give 'em that slow music, and they likely to just fall asleep before we can even get 'em upstairs with a girl. Don't nobody make no money then."

Leona looked down, hurt. "That slow music's the blues, Miss Mamie. I thought the men liked it."

Mamie reached out and stroked Leona's wrist. "They do, honey, but it's not good for business. Now, I could get me somebody from town to play the piano, play them nice fast tunes; might not be so good as you, but I wouldn't have to give 'em room and board, neither."

Leona had felt a cold chill settle into her then. She'd known for a time this was coming, but she'd hoped she might have a little longer. Just long enough to save for a ticket to Chicago or Atlanta and a couple of months of room and board while she tried to get a job singing, maybe even make a record of her own...

Miss Mamie had taken a last pull off her cigarette, then stubbed it out in a china plate. "I love you like my own, Leona, you know that; I done raised you since before you could put two words together. But you need to be makin' a decision: Either you stay here and take up The Life, or you move on."

Miss Mamie had gotten up then and left.

Beulah, the cook, had worked over the stove in the corner, listening quietly. She was a kind woman who came out here, to the edge of the bayou, every day to work for Miss Mamie. She'd never minded that Leona slept in the kitchen, and kept her phonograph there; she liked the music, too, and she liked Leona.

She'd waited until Mamie had gone, then she'd come over to where Leona sat, wiping furiously at her tears. "Don't cry, honey," she'd said, in her soft, sweet voice. "You can sing just as good as any of 'em, just as good as Ma or

Bessie or Victoria Spivey. You don't need this place."

Leona had looked up at Beulah gratefully. "You think so?"

"I know so," Beulah had said, giving her a hug that smelled like warm cornbread. "The only men you need to make money is the kind that'll let you sing, and you'll make a lot more money than you'd make here. You believe that."

Leona wished she could.

She tried to imagine herself saying yes, going into one of the upstairs bedrooms with Jackson Smith, who would be sweaty and smell like machine oil and liquor, and feeling his rough hands on her skin. She tried to imagine doing that every night, doing that five or ten times a night, until she was too old and none of the men wanted her.

Leona felt something hot on her cheek, and realized she was crying again. She brushed the tears away, angry at herself. It was a simple decision.

Stay or go.

Sing the blues...or live them.

The song finished, and Leona lifted the needle off the record. She was about to play it again when she heard something out in the brush, near the edge of the swamp.

"Lumpy?" she called out, hoping to see the mangy old cat scamper up.

Instead, she spotted a light bobbing among the trees, nearing. A few seconds later the lantern rounded a big mangrove, and Leona saw it was—

"Lizzie!"

She started to smile and was about to dart forward, when she saw Lizzie stop about thirty feet away.

"That you, Leona?"

Something was wrong with Lizzie.

Even from this distance, Leona could see her pale smock—usually spotless—was spotty and stained, and the night breeze took on a terrible scent, something spoke of death and terror, as it passed over Lizzie.

"It's me, Lizzie. Is somethin' wrong—?"

Lizzie took a few more steps forward. "Anybody else out here?"

Leona shook her head. "No'm, just us."

"Good."

Lizzie reached her now, and Leona actually gasped. The older woman was covered in bloodstains, and there were long scratch marks on her hands and arms, marks that were just barely scabbed over. Her left hand was also burned, and Leona saw pink flesh and white blisters.

And the smell nearly made Leona gag.

"What that smell, Lizzie?"

"Leona, honey, can you do me a favor? Bring some warm water, a towel, some new clothes. I can't let nobody else see me like this. Can you do that for me?"

Leona couldn't stop staring. "Should I get the doctor?"

"No, that's...that's not my blood. It's Lumpy's."

Leona placed that awful odor now: She'd smelled it once when Lumpy had lost part of an ear in a fight with a raccoon, and he'd somehow covered himself in this acrid fear scent.

"Lumpy...?"

Lizzie made a fluttering motion with her hands. "Oh honey, we'll talk about that ol' cat later. Can you just get me those things now?"

Leona nodded and ran off.

Five minutes later she had a pail of warm water, towels and a new dress. She stood by as Lizzie stripped out of the remains of her old clothes, and started to towel that smell off her skin.

"What happened to Lumpy?"

"I'm sorry, Leona, I know you liked that critter, but he's dead now. Just as well, anyway—cat's bad luck in a whorehouse."

"Dead?" Leona actually flinched from the news.

Lizzie looked at the girl carefully. "Leona, honey, can you keep a secret?"

Leona nodded, but she was already starting to suspect this was one secret she wasn't about to much like.

"All right. Remember I told you about that hoodoo man I met in New Orleans? Well, he gave me some secrets."

"Secrets...?"

"He told me how to call the Devil."

Leona gaped for a moment, then stifled a laugh. If she didn't believe in Jacky-Ma-Lantern, she didn't see much reason to believe in the Devil, either.

"Don't laugh, child. I did it, and it worked."

Leona made an exaggerated gesture of looking around. "Where is he, Lizzie? I don't see me no Devil."

Lizzie ignored her. "Here's what that hoodoo man told me: On Hallow's Eve, he said, you needs a black cat. You boil that animal alive, then you take the bones and wash 'em in a spring, until the Devil comes to you. Then you can ask him for whatever you want."

Leona suddenly realized the meaning of the scratches, the blood and the burns on Lizzie's arms, of the kettle that Beulah had seen Lizzie leave with in the afternoon, and the knowledge staggered her. "Oh lawd, Lizzie...you boiled that poor animal alive..."

"Leona, that cat was so old he couldn't even catch him a horsefly no more."

"But that...that ain't right..."

"Right or not, honey—it *worked*. I boiled him near that spring out in the woods, the one not far from ol' Guffey's farm, then I washed those bones in that spring, and I looked up...and sure 'nough, I seen this man walkin' up to me. He asked what I was wantin', and I tol' him."

Leona asked, "What'd you say?"

Lizzie finished washing, and started shrugging into the

new dress. "I tol' him I wanted a rich man to come and love me and take me out of this place, far away. And he said it'd happen tonight."

Leona guffawed. "You can't believe that—"

Lizzie finished straightening out the dress. "I can believe it. It's happenin' right now." She walked up to Leona and gave her a small kiss on the cheek, and whispered, "You 'bout the only part of Mamie's I'll miss."

Then she walked past Leona, into the house.

Leona stood for a moment, shocked, unable to move.

She toed at the tattered dress Lizzie had left on the ground, trying not to imagine Lumpy being forced into a boiling kettle, screaming in agony as Lizzie held him down...

She shook the pictures out of her head, then turned and walked back into the house.

She was just leaving the kitchen and heading for the piano in the front parlor when Miss Mamie's bustled up. "There you are, child! We've got johns, and we need some music. And for lawd's sake, try to play somethin' lively!"

"Yes, Miss Mamie."

Leona hurried to the piano, and glanced towards the bar, where there stood only a single customer. He was leaning across the mahogany counter, chatting idly to Harold while his drink was fixed. He wore a spotless, expensive suit and hat in the most current style, in a pale pastel color. His hair was neatly pommaded into curls, and his posture and build shouted confidence and money. When he turned to glance back towards the piano for a moment, Leona's breath caught in her throat.

He was without question the handsomest man she'd ever seen. He grinned as he saw her, with his liquid brown eyes and perfect jawline and gleaming teeth.

Miss Mamie was fawning over this newcomer, plainly sensing the money as well, and just before she sat down to play, Leona overheard the name "Lizzie."

She was into the third bar of Sippie Wallace's "Jack of Diamond Blues" when Lizzie entered the bar and sidled up to the stranger, smiling. Leona couldn't hear their conversation, but it was only a few seconds before Lizzie cried out, ecstatic, leapt up from her bar stool, gave the stranger a brief kiss and then ran from the room.

The stranger smiled after her, and then turned that look on Leona.

And in that instant Leona's fingers failed her, because she knew who the stranger was, and she knew that Lizzie had told her the truth.

"Leona, honey, play somethin' happy," Miss Mamie called to her, still grinning at the fine-looking man. "Looks like Lizzie done gone and got herself a marriage proposal."

Leona tried to smile, but it was a weak attempt. She tried to remember one of the rags she'd heard on a trip to the music store last month, but it came out sounding melancholy.

Leona saw Miss Mamie bustle from the room, and realized it was just her, Harold the bartender, and the stranger now. She felt his eyes on her, and tried to look down only at her hands, moving across the keys, trying to find the sprightly melody that was hidden somewhere inside the tune—

"Why don't you play something you can sing to?"

Leona started to reply, happened to glance back—and froze, her jaw hanging open like a cartoon character.

The handsome black man was gone; the man who had just spoken to her was white, mid-thirties, wearing a pin-striped suit.

"I heard you can sing pretty good," he said, resting an elbow on the top of the piano, grinning down at her.

"I...ain't so good," Leona said, not because she believed it, but because she didn't want to talk to him, no matter what color he was.

The Bad Man.

"C'mon, now, girl, you act like it's a sin to sing."

"Might be," Leona said. Her palms felt sweaty, and she could hear her heart thumping faster than a rag rhythm.

He shrugged, and took a step back. "Guess I got the wrong girl. See, I'm scouting for the Toby. You know what that is?"

"Yes, sir, I knows." Lizzie'd once had a john who played fiddle for Butterbeans and Suzie, and Lizzie had made sure he talked to Leona all about "riding the Toby", or traveling the circuit put together by the Theatre Owners' Booking Association. The fiddler had told her horror stories about being stranded in towns without hotels for coloreds, and dealing with theatre owners who charged performers three times what a meal anywhere else would cost...but he'd laughed as he told his tales, and Leona could tell he wouldn't give up that fiddle for anything.

And it was sure better than working for Miss Mamie. Leona dreamed of a day when people came to listen to *her*, not just be entertained until they could get a girl to take them upstairs.

"I'm looking for new performers. Heard through the grapevine that there was a colored girl working in some backwoods whorehouse who'd knock my socks off. But, if that's not you..."

"It's me."

What if he really *was* a booking agent for the Toby? Could she afford to pass up what might be her only chance? And if he wasn't - if he really was the Devil himself—then she'd sing like heaven for him, and give him a case of the blues he'd never get over.

He chuckled, amused, then said, "So sing for me."

She thought for a moment, and remembered Beulah telling her that she sang "Hard Time Blues" even better than Ida Cox. She picked out the opening notes on the piano, then let the pain and fear and humiliation and sadness explode deep inside her, until all the emotions could only be channeled up through her throat and out through her words, released into the world.

I never seen such a real hard time before,
I never seen such a real hard time before,
The wolf keeps walking all round my door.

All thoughts of where she was and who she was playing for vanished as she gave herself, body and soul, to the song. She closed her eyes and just felt and played, and when she finished she knew she'd never sung that well before. She was drained, covered in sweat and tears, weary with a bone-deep exhaustion she'd never felt before.

The sound of slow applause drew her back.

She wiped at her eyes and turned to see the white man slowly clapping. He finished and half-collapsed onto the piano.

"Lord, girl, they weren't just whistling Dixie. I do believe you may be even better than Bessie or Ma. You could make somebody a lot of money, you know that?"

Leona should have been pleased, but right now all she wanted was the comfort of her little pallet in the kitchen's warm pantry.

The agent stepped closer, bending over her in what he probably hoped was some sort of intimate, even fatherly, gesture. "It really takes it out of you, don't it?"

Leona just nodded.

"You're too damn good to be stuck in this place. That Miss Mamie, she's okay, but she don't realize what she's got in you. You need to be on the circuit. We can start you touring, just a few of the smaller theaters first, maybe opening for one of the bigger acts, then we move you up on the bill, get you bigger venues, start recording. How'd you like to see your name on a number-one record?"

Leona finally risked a glance up at him, and offered a shy smile. "That'd be fine, mister."

He laughed. "Atta girl. Okay, so let's make a deal, you and me."

Leona's fatigue was suddenly replaced with a numbing dread. "A...deal...?"

"Sure. Always gotta do the paperwork."

He reached into a pocket and pulled forth a few sheets of folded paper and a pen. "Standard contract. All you have to do is sign, then I'll make your arrangements. In twenty-four hours you'll be on a train to Atlanta, ready to play the 81 Theater."

Leona knew that wasn't possible; no real booking agent could get anyone into Atlanta's biggest theater in a day. At least no *human* booking agent.

"You're him, aren't you?"

"Who?"

Leona couldn't bring herself to say the usual names; she settled on the one from the Jacky-Ma-Lantern story. "The Bad Man."

She looked up now to see him squinting down at her. He didn't look like the Devil—no red skin, no horns, no pointed ears or tail. He looked like what he said he was.

And yet...there was something in his eyes, something that wasn't right. She suddenly knew this—*thing*—standing over her was ancient, and intelligent, and wanted her soul.

"C'mon, Leona, what's worse: Me giving you the life you deserve, or Miss Mamie wanting to make you part of The Life that killed your mama?"

Leona didn't answer, didn't move. She got the impression that the lights had gone down around her. In an instant of panic she looked up for Harold, but couldn't see the bar in the sudden gloom. She wasn't even sure she could find her way out of this room now.

"Look what I'm doing for Lizzie: Giving her a fine, rich, handsome husband. She's going to be happy, Leona. You could be, too."

"Lizzie called you here tonight?"

He cocked one shoulder in a half-motion of apology. "Yes, and I know you liked that old cat, so I'm sorry about that, but sometimes the rituals must be...obeyed."

"And what you want from me?"

"You know, Leona. It's the usual transaction."

Leona whispered, "My soul."

He murmured in agreement, and then just stood there, looking at her.

Leona slid just far enough away from him that she could stand to look up, into his old, old eyes. "But how would I sing?"

He looked back at her, and Leona saw the first sign of doubt on his face, a crack in his confidence. "You'll still sing just as well, your voice will still be yours—"

Leona dared to cut him off. "But the voice ain't nothin' without the soul."

"It won't matter. You'll be famous and rich anyway."

"It'll matter to *me*."

He seemed to gain several inches in height, and the lights grew even dimmer, until his pale white face was all Leona could see.

"So, what—you'd rather be working here, letting Jackson Smith grind into you, or worse—how about Parson Mills? He must weigh—what, three, four hundred pounds? How'd you like to have that on top of you, Leona, pounding away at you, and all so's you can make fifty cents, and get on with the next customer? Is that what you want?"

Leona's face grew hot, and her eyes filled with tears again. "No, but I—"

"But you WHAT?!" He was furious now, and Leona half-expected to see him start spitting brimstone sparks.

"You really think you can get out of here some other way? I got news for you, honey: You're good, but you're not *that* good. You'd just be one more little colored girl trying to hustle up jobs until you get forced to be some white lady's maid to earn a dollar, or worse—wind up as a crib whore in some house that'll make Miss Mamie's look like the Ritz. Hell's gonna look pretty Goddamn fine after what life's got in store for you, girly."

Suddenly something changed in Leona, something she'd kept carefully tamped down erupted out, and she let it. She was on her feet and shouting into his moon-like face:

"Let me tell you somethin,' mister: I know how good I can sing, and I know there's lots of white men and colored men both who'll try to take advantage of me. But maybe I'm smarter than you give me credit for, and maybe I don't mind hard work and some heartache, because I'm already pretty used to it. So maybe the best thing you can do right now is get outta my way and let me leave here on my own two feet."

Leona walked by him, and the room was there again, and Harold was staring at her as she walked by him, her face still wet but determined.

"Leona...?"

She ignored him.

It took her maybe two minutes to rush to the pantry, and pack everything she owned into a burlap potato sack. If Lumpy were still alive, she would've taken him, too.

As it was, she'd leave alone. She'd managed to save up nearly ten dollars from tips over the last year, and she thought it might be enough to get her a train ticket to Atlanta, or maybe New Orleans.

She walked back through the parlor, towards the front door. Miss Mamie was there, staring at her.

"Child, what —?!"

Leona silenced her with a quick kiss, and a goodbye. "I'm sorry, Miss Mamie. You been kind to me, and I 'preciate it, but I got to go."

"Tonight?"

Leona nodded, and headed for the front door—

—where the Bad Man stood, waiting.

"You sure you want to go that way? Even if you do get to the city, you know what to do when you get there?" Now his laughter was a hollow, bad sound. "You're just like a rabbit runnin' right into the coon dog's mouth."

"Get out of my way," Leona said.

He didn't move. "Last chance, Leona. I won't come to you again, no matter how bad it gets. You're liable to be wishing you could conjure me back up a month from now. If you even get that far; it's a bad night, tonight. Lots of things out there in the dark that'd find you mighty tasty."

Leona looked straight at him as she reached for the doorknob. "Can't be nothin' worse out there'n what's in here."

He let her go.

Without another word she strode out the front door, down the steps, and onto the soft dirt trail that eventually led to town, five miles on. He was right, of course; it was dangerous to walk this path at night, with everything from snakes to robbers about.

Somehow Leona didn't think they'd trouble her.

There was a railway station in town, and she thought the first train came about sunrise. She'd be on it, no matter where it was headed.

She cradled the burlap sack in her arms, and started to sing to herself as she walked into the warm Hallowe'en night, away from Miss Mamie's, never looking back.

WORTH THE HAVING

By Michael Paul Gonzalez

How does it feel?

It asks this as it cuts deep into the inner thigh, flesh and fat zippering apart, its tongue probing into the fresh wound.

How are you doing?

The thing wouldn't want an answer even if there was one. It only wants screams.

This is going to be worth it. You're going to love next year. This will make it worth the having.

I used to wonder what could be worth this. The heat of its palms pushing legs apart. The cold, slow rivulets of saliva dripping down like icy syrup, washed away with slowing pulses of hot blood. That single tooth in its lower jaw, barbed and curved. That awful, knowing smile from the puckered sphincter of its mouth. This year, I finally understand that phrase, *worth the having*. This year, the final year of our horrible agreement—the thing still uses that word, *agreement*, as if I wanted any of this—I understand it all.

Twenty-two years ago, I cut across the backyard of Mikey Slater's dad's house. This was the night before Halloween; the night, I'd later learn, that the thing would stretch its legs and go for a walk. The thing was the reason for the season, the whole tradition of Halloween had started because of it. Masks, costumes, disguises, none of it for fun. All of it primal camouflage to help the prey hide from the predator.

Nobody remembers that part of the tradition anymore. Not even the thing itself. It just knows to walk the night before Halloween. And it walks to me. I don't ask where it goes when it leaves me or what it does on Halloween night. I'm just glad it's gone.

Anyway, Mikey Slater. His parents had been divorced a few years, and I treated our hangout like a second home. The other bonus was that it was a quick end-around the neighborhood when I needed to get home fast. I was on my way home from checking out Mikey's Halloween costume at his mom's house and had about two minutes to get home before dinner was cold and my ass would get spanked.

We'd made a pact to dress as characters from this cartoon about interstellar knights. We had some great things rigged to our costumes, lights and fake swords, the whole works. We expected that tomorrow night, we'd barely be able to do any trick or treating since we'd be mobbed by admirers wondering how we obtained these amazing costumes.

I vaulted the six foot wooden, slatted fence, landed soft in the garden, not caring if my presence was announced or not, since Mikey's dad never cared if I cut through.

And then I saw Mr. Slater lying in the grass near the backdoor, naked. Another person straddled him, pinning his arms down. Pale skin, soft curves, it looked like a woman. The back did, anyway. The head was too small, and bald with a Mohawk of downy feathers. This thing, this silhouette dipped down, the head bobbing just above Mr. Slater's crotch. I was young, but not so young that I didn't have a small clue about what I might be seeing.

I heard a whisper, *Almost done, almost done. Next year is going to be fantastic. This will all be worth it.*

And Mr. Slater replied, "No, no, no. No more. There's

nothing I want. Everything I want is gone..." Occasionally he hissed, his breath, stifling a scream.

Pleasure wasn't part of this.

"No more! No more, please!"

You must want something. It's you and I forever. If you don't want anything...

And here the thing yanked a hand back from Mr. Slater's thigh, and that's when I noticed the blood, and the flap of flayed skin that I'd initially mistaken for underwear pulled down.

I tried to turn around, grabbed the fence to bail out. I wanted to get out of there, wanted to be home.

You...want?

It whipped its head around at me, and I felt its voice in my head more than I heard it.

"Take him! Take him!" Mr. Slater cried out, pointing at me.

I can't explain any of what happened next. Can't explain the face I saw when I locked eyes with the thing. Can't explain the speed with which it moved. It crossed the yard in three hitching strides, seizing my ankle as I tried to get out of the yard. I flopped my upper body over the fence and struggled for anything to grab, to pull, to get free.

I heard a whisper...no, felt it.

Mine.

One quick bite on my ankle. A burning pain, searing, electric.

Make a wish before you go to bed. Think about what you want next year more than anything. We have an agreement now.

It wasn't a question or an offer.

It released me and I dropped to the ground in the alley behind the fence.

I reached to my ankle. There was a fading flash of pain and burning, but no blood. No cut.

Mikey's dad came stumbling around the corner, wearing nothing but a pair of shorts, holding a handgun. "Is it still here? Is it?"

I said nothing. What could I say? What the hell was happening?

"My God, if you hadn't shown up...I'd...I'm free." He smiled at me and turned away. There was a flash in his eyes, a moment where he was teetering between life and death, that gun the fulcrum between finishing something very bad or starting something new. His hand rose slowly.

"But, don't, Mikey..." Those were the only three words in the mess behind my lips that could break through. It was enough. His hand swung free and heavy.

"I'm sorry. I'm so sorry. Try to...just...try to think of good things for yourself." He looked at the gun again. "Heh. What the hell was I gonna do with this thing? Don't ever think about trying to kill it, whatever you do. Just take what you have coming and then think of good things for yourself."

I barely remembered getting home. By the time I was through my front door, the details were hazy. My ankle was fine. No cut, no scab, not even a scratch. I slid into bed, trying to remember the thing, the face, the hands, anything, but it was all gone. A haze. My gaze drifted over the shelves around my room, the random toys scattered around, the baseball bat leaning against the corner. I hopped out of bed and brought it close by, feeling like it would keep me safe, not knowing from what. As I drifted off that night, my last thought was about Little League and my wish that I wasn't too damn fat to play shortstop.

That's good enough. A whisper, shot through the center of my brain.

Cold sweat broke over my upper lip, then calmness, then sleep.

When I woke up the next morning, I'd forgotten the

previous night completely. I was full of energy, light on my feet. I felt ready to take on the world. Things felt a little darker in the afternoon as I walked by Mr. Slater's house on my way to Mikey's, but I couldn't quite peg why. I saw him sitting on his porch, a strange smile on his face. I kept moving, and that night was a Halloween much like any other.

The following year I dropped a lot of weight. Got faster. Made the team. Didn't think of how or why, just attributed it to hard work and eating right.

Then early October came and I found the postcard on my pillow when I got home from school. I'd like to say I got cold chills when I picked it up, or that it felt like flesh or leathery hide, but no, just plain, cheap cardboard. Typed in a neat white font on one side, it read:

Halloween is almost here. Did you have a good year? What do you want next year? Think hard! Make it worth the having.

I wanted to show the card to my mom, but by the time she got home from work, it was gone. Every time anyone brought up Halloween, this icicle of dread would rocket down my spine, and then disappear in a haze of thoughts about candy and costumes, an itch at the back of my mind that I couldn't quite scratch.

The night before Halloween, laying my costume out before going to bed, my only thoughts were on candy and sneaking around in the dark. It was two in the morning when I woke to a great weight on top of me, pushing the blankets down tight and cocooning me inside. I opened my eyes to see a silhouette, slight shoulders that were a bit too sharp, full breasts that seemed too round, slender arms that pinned me down. It was too dark to see details. I tried to cry out for my parents, but the thing lifted a hand to my mouth, cold boneless fingers clamping down. The palm spread like cold jelly as the thing drew its palm back, forcing one, then two fingers into my mouth. There was a texture to the bottom of them, something between a snake's belly and octopus suction pads.

Shhhhh...

The whisper in my brain.

Have you thought on it?

Thought on what?

The postcard I sent. What you want for next year.

Who are you?

It doesn't matter who I am. It matters who you are. You are mine.

How did you—

Just as you hear me in your mind, I hear you in mine. You are mine.

What does that mean?

It means you are mine.

I felt the thing rock down with its pelvis, grind into my stomach.

The agreement is not without benefit to you.

I didn't agree to anything.

Does a fish agree to feed a shark? Does a tree agree to be struck by lightning? You are mine.

The thing drew closer to me, and I squeezed my eyes shut. Everything grew bright, until I could make out shapes, then colors. Then I could see it in front of me.

You don't need your ears to hear me, nor your eyes to see. You are mine.

It was mottled and gray. The torso was curved and sensuous, but the head, that too-small head. The puckered sphincter of a mouth that prolapsed in and out, exposing that single jagged tooth. The two giant eyes, bulbous and red, shot with veins but no pupils, the two smaller green eyes in between. No ears. No nose. The tuft of white feathers in a stripe over the shining bald skull. Squeezing my eyes shut tighter only seemed to draw out more clarity.

You need to understand how this works. I will show you. Think of a woman you desire.

I couldn't. I was twelve. There wasn't desire yet, only a strange fascination. An occasional stirring if I saw a woman on TV in a swimsuit or that time I sneaked a peek at my dad's private magazine collection—

The thing on top of me changed. Hair grew. The head filled in. The face melted and morphed into the perfectly sculpted features of that lady from *Beach Patrol* who had just done the cover shoot for Playboy. Bronze skin. Swaying breasts. A sculpted collarbone. Skin coated in a sheen of sweat, just as I'd seen her in the centerfold.

Better?

It hadn't changed the feeling of the fingers in my mouth, cold like snails, twitching and probing around my tongue.

Every year on this night, I'm going to find you. I must feed. In exchange, you will tell me something you want, and over the course of the next year, you shall have it.

But I don't want—

You are—and the fingers extended slowly, pushing against the back of my throat, gagging me—*mine. Understand it. Tell me your desire. Make it worth the having.*

I want you to leave.

Not part of the bargain. Not your place to ask. You are mine.

The fingers pushed deeper still until I could feel them sliding down into my throat. I couldn't breathe. Instinct kicked in and I began to thrash. I needed to escape. I bit down hard on the fingers, breaking the skin, cold peppery ichor oozing into my mouth.

The thing didn't draw back. It moaned. Reached up its other hand and caressed itself.

More.

It pushed hard on my mouth, wanting me to bite. I let my jaw go slack. It sighed, the kind of sigh I was too young to understand as sexually frustrated, and its fingers pulled back.

I felt my lungs suck in air. I thought I was going to die. Thoughts of school crossed my mind. Thoughts of family trips I'd never get to take. I'd never get to see Disney World—

Is that something you desire?

I nodded in spite of myself. The thing on top of me slowly morphed back to its original form, spinning around on my body so I could only see its back. I felt it pulling at the sheets covering my feet.

I want you to think harder next year. Make it good. Make it worth the having. This is scarcely worth a toe, let alone two.

"What, what—"

And I felt the cold fingers of one hand clamp down on my ankle while the other fingers slithered between my toes, constricting them, spreading them apart.

"No," I said. "Nononono please don't—"

Next year you will remember this and understand what it means when I say make it worth the having.

Its head lowered and its lips wrapped around my big toe. It sucked once, twice, then clamped down with a force I can't describe. That single tooth razored into the meat of my toe and flicked, cutting, tearing. I screamed. I had to have screamed, but there was no sound. I could feel the blood pumping out of my toe, feel the vibration of serrated tooth on bone; clamping, twisting, pulling, until it was all electricity and cold air. The thing turned to me and pursed its lips. It showed me my toe, sucking it so it bobbed in and out of its mouth before tipping its head back and swallowing. The opening between its legs pulsed and shuddered, cold slime pooling onto my sheets. It sighed.

One more.

This time I did get a scream out, a small yelp as it

latched onto my second toe and began chewing again. Its leg cracked and bent around at an impossible angle until its foot was over my mouth, spreading like taffy, covering my nose and lips so that no sound could escape, no breath could enter. There was no smell, just electric pain, vibrant agony.

A crack, a tear, and more cold air. The second toe went much easier than the first. The creature arched its back and swallowed, ripples shivering down its flanks as it came again. It spun, bringing its face close to mine. I squeezed my eyes shut to no effect.

Enjoy your trip. Next year, think harder.

Without moving its torso, it raised one leg, stretched it toward my window sill. Gripping hard, it pulled itself up and out into the night.

I stared down over my soaked sheets at my foot. The silhouette in the dark room danced through the purple lightning of pain. It didn't seem to be bleeding. It didn't hurt. I didn't pass out from the pain. I passed out when I tried to count my toes and had to stop at three.

I awoke screaming as I felt someone shaking my shoulder. Unbidden, I saw that face, round and leathery and purple, hovering inches from mine.

"Honey, it's okay!"

When I opened my eyes I saw my mother's face.

"Are you feeling okay? Your bed is soaked. Did you wet the bed?"

I burst into tears, kicking at the sheets until they came free. I could feel the burning sensation in my toes still, the raw wound scraping at the fabric.

"No!" I shouted. "Look what it did! Look what it did!"

I held my foot up. Five toes. Had I not already been crying, I might have started then. Or possibly even wet the bed out of sheer joy. I wiggled my toes. Jumped out of bed.

"What's gotten into you?"

My big toe was a bit red. My second toe had a definite hard ridge beneath the skin like a scar, but they were there. They were back. I was whole. My toes were—

Mine

Mine.

"Did you stub your toe last night?" My mom grabbed my foot, poking at my toes.

No pain.

"No, I'm...Ow!"

There was a scab on the underside of my big toe. Damp sheets. No blood. Five toes.

"You need to get up! And be more careful. You get a cut like that, you show me, okay? Otherwise it could get infected and you might lose your toes. You wouldn't want that, would you?"

I blanched.

"You need to get up. It's Halloween! Big breakfast to fuel up for a big night, right?"

Her hand sank into the dampness on my sheet, the essence that the creature had left behind in its ecstasy. Her eyes became vacant, distant, as she pulled the sheet off and bunched them on the floor.

"Well. I'll wash these later. You go run along." She absently licked at her fingers as she left.

By the time I made it downstairs for breakfast, I'd forgotten about my aching toes. By the time I was out the door, my sheets were in the wash and my mind was on Halloween.

The events of the evening never returned to traumatize me. I don't remember much of the school year that followed, but I remember our vacation. The best time we'd ever had as a family. I remember years later, my parents telling me that trip had been a new beginning for them, bringing them out of a rough patch that I had been blissfully unaware of.

The next year when Halloween drew close, I got another card, this time in my lunch box at school.

Matte black, bearing only the reminder: MAKE IT WORTH THE HAVING.

Reading those words instantly sent a spasm of pain through my foot and up my spine. I couldn't see the creature in mind, but it was omnipresent, that assault, that pain, and the reward it brought.

The night before Halloween that year, I asked if I could sleep in my parent's room. And as soon as the question left my mouth, a whisper buzzed through my brain—

Oh no, don't make them watch. Why would you do that to them?

So I didn't. I slept in my closet that year, thinking it might not find me, but I was wrong.

I could explain this. Break it down year by year and tell what happened, but that's not why I'm going to do. It's about that phrase, *Make It Worth the Having.*

That second time, it stood at the door of my closet, towering over me, taking on features it must have thought looked friendly, the face shifting from Santa Claus to Jesus to cartoon mice and rabbits.

I don't want you to go through this for nothing. Think big.

Please stop.

I'll stop when I'm full and finished and I'll still come back next year. Don't wish for toys. Don't wish for things for other people. Think of yourself. Remember our meeting last year, and know what's about to happen will be far worse than a few toes. Don't let this happen for nothing. Make it worth the—

I screamed hard, muffled by the gelatinous glob of fingers it had forced into my mouth again. I just wanted it to shut up. I never wanted to hear that phrase again, but I knew I would. I knew this, all of this, would be happening again, and again.

That's a big burden to put on the shoulders of a child, right? Have almost anything you want, in exchange for giving the thing what it wants. That's not accurate. In exchange for the thing *taking* what it wants. I mean, what can a child think of that would be worth that? The second year, all I could think of was sports cars. It made me try again—why ask for something I couldn't legally use? Millions of dollars? Same thing. It had to be personal. So the second year, I wished to be the fastest, strongest kid in my school.

Done.

And in exchange for that, for the next sixty minutes, the creature flayed my arms and legs with that horrible tooth, peeled back my skin and chose three strands of exposed muscle from each limb, snapping them near one tendon and pulling them out like spaghetti, lifting it as high as it would go before placing the strand in its mouth and sucking it down greedily, biting off the other end at the tendon. It held its gelatinous foot over my mouth the whole time, tiny suctioned footpads inhaling the screams that never made it into the night. Blood everywhere. Pain like I'd never felt, to that point anyway.

When it was done, it left me wide open like a biology class project pinned to a tray, trying to sleep and failing miserably. I passed out at some point and woke up in the morning, mildly sore but fully intact, testing out my new-found strength on my dad's weight bench by the end of the day. By the end of the week, I was running home from school without breaking a sweat. By the end of the school year, I was medaling in every sport I chose.

When October rolled around, and the black postcard fell out a library book I pulled from the shelf, the sinking dread in my stomach was almost matched by the excitement of the next thing I planned to ask for.

That night, it ate half of one my kidneys. Once it managed to pull the organ free it wasn't so bad, but getting there was sheer hell. Fourteen years old, I made the wish any hormonally rampaging boy would, and that year I got every girl I was interested in. Was it worth it? Hard to say. But that year I came to understand that I was addicted. That I understood what *worth the having* meant, and that my life was going to improve.

I thought I had it all figured out. I had to try something new, and something new, despite seeing the thing lick its lips, despite seeing the horrible tongue dance over that single stupid tooth in the puckered maw it called a mouth, something new was too enticing to resist. Year by year, piece by piece, I was going to become a better man.

Everything that's happened in my life is a bit of a blur, but not those nights. Those, I have perfect clarity on.

I got better-than-perfect eyesight the year it spent hours working my eyeballs free from the sockets after using one jagged nail to cut my eyelids off. More length and girth downstairs (it was my first year in college, after all), that year was sheer torture. It changed its shape to a calendar girl, arousing me, bringing me to climax orally in spite of myself, the soft supple features of the woman's body betrayed by the cold, slimy oatmeal feeling of the thing's mouth and throat. And then came the pain, my member first peeled like a raw potato with that single hooked tooth, then the soft tissue torn free, then the tongue probing into the open wound at my crotch until my testes were pulled free from my body and eaten—no, nibbled, held daintily between thumb and forefinger with pinky extended—until they were gone. That night I was on a camping trip, so the thing didn't even need to muffle my screams, and I obliged it until I was choking on my own vomit and my throat was raw. Physically, I was fine the next day, but it took me a few weeks to get the feeling of it all out of my mind. Once I did, I quickly developed a reputation as *Big Man on Campus* in every way imaginable. By the end of the year, every man and woman worth having knew my number.

After college, my life became career-oriented. Real Estate. Stock Market. Passive income. I wanted to be rich while having as much free time as possible to research, because I needed to know how to finish this thing. Mikey's Dad, all those years ago, had simply begged the creature to stop, and when it saw me, it did. I asked it one year if I could do the same thing. It only replied, *You are mine.*

I researched it through college and beyond, and when I had enough money to hire people, they researched it too. I couldn't be very specific with them about my reasons, of course, but I could offer grants to religious studies students, hire paranormal investigators, demonologists. Six solid years of research yielded nothing. Not a damn thing. Every ancient society, every dead culture I could study I did, end to end, to the extent that there was some buzz that I'd be nominated for a Nobel for advancing the studies so far. Nobody had heard of the thing. In college, I'd had the idea to go back and ask Mr. Slater about it, but he looked at me like I was crazy.

I wondered how much time it had spent with him, since his life wasn't so great. What if that was the first night he'd encountered it? What if the thing had been with him for years and was on a downswing, taking things away instead of granting them? I'd never know.

I was thirty five, with another Halloween approaching, a wife I loved and my first child on the way. And that was the final straw. I couldn't have this thing in my life with a child in the house. This year I was going to ask it for an exit.

This year, I received something worse than a black postcard in the mail. This year, the afternoon of what I'd come to think of as Visitation Night, we had to rush to the hospital. Complications. Our baby was lost. It made no sense. My wife was perfectly healthy, and everything had been going fine. But there was no heartbeat, no sign of life. My wife was inconsolable. She had to be sedated, and even as they were putting the IV into her, she was crying out, asking: *Will this hurt the baby? You can't give me these drugs. It'll cause complications...*

My wife refused treatment, insisted that they were mistaken. We went home, the doctor pulling me aside to suggest that we let her rest a few days, then discuss inducing labor to finish the procedure.

Finish the procedure. Just like that, our baby had somehow progressed from human being to benign growth. A mole to be scraped off. A boil to be lanced. All of those cardboard pumpkins hanging on the wall, smiling, calm. That stupid friendly skeleton on the door. They were the only witnesses.

That night, it came. Slow, silent, and sad-eyed. It sat at the foot of the couch, where I was sleeping. My wife wanted to be alone, and I didn't know what to do. I didn't notice that I'd drifted off to sleep, but one minute it wasn't there and then it was, laying a hand on my calf. I didn't feel fear. I only felt empty.

I am ready—

Just take something and go, I said.

I am ready to end our bargain.

I was speechless. It felt strange, another gut-punch, another loss, another branch pruned form the tree of my life. I wanted to dictate terms. I wanted a safe exit, but once the baby was gone...I wanted it back. I wanted it to continue. I needed it, this thing, this surety.

I will give you your child.

What?

I will give you your child. I will take it. I will be the surrogate. Tomorrow, you will be a father.

It wasn't a question or an offer.

"But my wife can't—"

She will remember nothing.

"I don't want this. You can't have it—my child. You can't. It's done."

Have I ever asked your permission for anything? The bargain ends because I say so. You are mine. Tomorrow you will be a father.

It led me to the bedroom. Made me open the door. Made sure my wife...I can't describe the look I saw on her face, how she instinctively curled her arms over her stomach, how her feral glare burned through me until *it* came into the room. Then she froze, and softened, and looked at me, her lower jaw working, trying to get out a question, to ask me what was happening.

It mounted her, stretched its arms out and wrapped those rubbery, cold fingers around her wrists, pinned her legs down, didn't bother to cover her mouth, because there was nobody to disturb with her screams. All I could do was watch. I knew what it felt like. I knew *exactly* what she was going through. I chuckled in spite of myself that she'd never be able to hold the pain of this childbirth over my head.

That single tooth tore her nightshirt open. That sphincter mouth traced kisses down her collarbone, between her breasts, suckling at her nipples until milk started to flow. Then it moved lower, elbows and shoulders dislocating so that it could keep her pinned down. Not that she was fighting at this point, only staring at me with wide eyes, panting for air until the thing's mouth reached her thighs.

How does it feel?

It asks this as it cuts deep into the inner thigh, flesh and fat zippering apart, its tongue probing into the fresh wound.

How are you doing?

The thing wouldn't want an answer even if there was one. It only wants screams.

This is going to be worth it. You're going to love next year. This will make it worth the having.

Its head stretched thin, narrowing impossibly at the mouth, the entire face a tubular beak, a hard proboscis that poked at her vulva until it found its way inside. She screamed then, my wife.

I could do nothing but watch it root, the heat of its palms pushing her legs apart. The cold, slow rivulets of saliva dripping down her sides like icy syrup, washed away with the regular and slowing pulses of her hot blood.

That single tooth in its lower jaw, barbed and curved, that awful knowing smile from the pucker of its mouth as it comes up for air, slowly retracting its head to stare at me, neck bent round the wrong way, slime coating its face, it made that hideous ring-mouth into an imitation of a smile.

It's a boy.

It plunged its beak into her stomach, slicing through skin, and fat, and muscle, splaying her open. Cold, gray slime oozed down her, mixing and pooling with her blood. That ringing, that ringing in my ears isn't ringing. It's her screaming. Screaming for the baby, screaming *no*, screaming my name, cursing me, damning me. Cursing the thing, even as it lowered its face to her flayed abdomen and forced its head inside.

Its back lurched up once, twice, as if taking great gulping swallows, and then it came, orgasmic shudders rippling through its spine as it straightened and stood up from the bed, staring at me, one hand cupping its swollen belly. It caressed my cheek, pushed a finger inside my mouth, pressed until my knees buckled. It lowered me onto the bed beside my wife. Tears streamed from her eyes, her organs warm and wet against my stomach. I reached out to her, stupidly, tried to cradle her in my arms.

The thing stood above us and arched its back, convulsing, straining, eyes swelling until the veins that laced them burst and bloody tears flowed. It straddled her, crouching lower and lower until it positioned its vagina above my wife's open torso. It pushed, pushed until it came...until...a child came. A membranous sac, slid out of its dilated opening and landed inside my wife. I saw through the pale pink membrane his face, calm and serene, sleeping.

Sleeping.

I woke to her screams, my wife clutching my arm, saying, "It's time! Holy shit it's time. They were wrong! My water broke! Do you feel it?"

I climbed from the bed, soaked, but not in her blood, but amniotic fluid. Aside from that, the sheets were clean in a way my memory could never be.

And we drove to the hospital, and I strode through the doors like a champion, pushing her wheelchair through the throng gathered there. I stared at the confused faces of the nurses and doctors and told them it was time.

They checked signs. They double checked charts. They made me sign waivers promising not to sue over all of this stillbirth confusion. "These things happen sometimes. We will of course be paying you for your pain and suffering in exchange for—"

I told them to shut the fuck up and do their job. We could discuss it later. There would be a later. There would be a rest of our lives. That's all that mattered.

You are all that mattered. Our son. My son. Mine.

I'm telling you all of this now before you understand it, because I never want you to hear it again. I never want you to know about any of this. It's gone. It's gone and it won't come back. It always keeps its promises. You're in my arms, with your perfect eyes, your ruddy cheeks, and I love you. More than anything. More than everything. I'm laughing at your gurgles, your tiny nose twitching, your perfect little ruby lips when they stretch into that smile, that same kind of goofy smile your mother gets. Your happy little gummy mouth that looks perfect. Perfect and normal except for that one thing that confused the doctors.

That single, smooth tiny tooth breaking through your lower gums. Doctors say this isn't unusual, they call them natal teeth. I know better. You yawn wide, showing me that tiny ivory blade, and you stare at me placidly, and I can only think.

Worth the having.

DONUTS

By Hal Bodner

Frederick opened the door and stepped onto his porch to find two zombies waiting. Their flesh-rotted arms reached for him while they moaned "Braaaaains!" in sepulchral tones. He brandished his machete and watched them cower in fear. When he was finished teasing the foul minions of the undead, he held out the plastic pumpkin. Greedy little hands with blackened fingernails and horrific, bloody wounds reached into the bucket and emerged with fists full of candy.

"Trick or treat!" they cried and dashed happily down the front path, leaving Frederick with a couple of Snickers Bites and a smattering of Hershey's Kisses rattling in the bottom of the bucket.

"That's all for this year, folks," he told the night air and retreated into his house.

He tossed the plastic machete into the corner next to the toy chain saw and the plastic hammer and stake. Depending on which costumes showed up at his door, he liked to be prepared. There were no toy guns though, in spite of the old silver bullet legend. Too many of them had been taken for real and he had no desire to end up as a statistic because some parent waiting for their little Wolfman-clad urchins to return to the car mistook his spray painted Super-Soaker for an AK47.

With only a little guilt, Frederick ate the last two Snickers. While he munched, he flipped the sign he hung in the window every Halloween so that the side reading *Sorry. Out of candy!* was facing the path, and left the overhead porch light on so any latecomers could see it. His timing had been perfect this year; he'd bought just enough candy to last until bedtime.

Yawning, he made for the stairs and frowned when the doorbell rang again. There were always one or two stragglers who overlooked the sign. Hopefully, there wouldn't be too many more so he could get to sleep without the constant ringing.

"Happy Halloween."

He was sorry now that he'd eaten the candy bars. Three small children stood on the porch, their faces hopeful beneath some pretty damned impressive make-up, and he felt bad that he had so little to offer them.

"I don't have much candy left," he explained as he upended the few remaining Kisses into their bags. "It's been a busy Halloween this year. I'm sorry. Actually," he added as something occurred to him, "maybe I *do* have something in the kitchen. Hang on and I'll be right back."

Three eager little faces gazed up at him, adorably expectant. Three little monsters of unidentifiable lineage, one green, one purple, and one orange.

He zipped into the kitchen and returned with a box of donuts. They weren't much, but they were all the sweets he had left in the house. Hopefully, the kids wouldn't be too disappointed.

"Here you go!" He held out the open box. "There's just enough for everyone to take two and still leave one for my breakfast tomorrow. Go ahead."

"Donuts?" said the little green one, the tallest of the three. "We get up here one freaking day of the year, and you give us *donuts*?"

"Shoulda had more chocolate Kisses, Dude," the orange

one chimed in. He was a little plumper and wore a pair of flower-print surfer shorts. "Donuts are definitely *not* cool."

Taken aback by their rudeness, Frederick stammered, "I...I...I beg your pardon?" Before he had a chance to slam the door in their ill-mannered little faces, they barged into the house.

"Now look here..."

He began the reprimand but stopped short, stunned. In the few steps between the front porch and the living room, the three children had...changed. Where before they were simply kids in elaborate make-up, now they were clearly something other than human.

The scaly green one was the tallest, standing almost as high as Frederick's chest. He was very thin and his face looked like someone had stacked a bunch of triangles together and added the features as an afterthought. His arms and legs were impossibly thin and seemed jointed in too many of the wrong places. He looked a bit like an alligator and a bit like a Praying mantis and a bit like an emaciated cucumber.

The tiniest, the little purple one, had come out in pink and turquoise spots and her eyes had grown huge upon her face. She—for Frederick got the distinct impression that it was a little girl—was still quite adorable. Then, the creature yawned and displayed an impressive array of shark-like teeth that audibly clashed together when she once again shut her mouth.

The one wearing the surfer shorts resembled an overgrown orange-colored pear. Shirtless, he had a thin chest and a bulbous pot belly that jiggled when he walked. Though his face was alien, the air of affected boredom was too obvious to be overlooked.

"One stinkin' day," Greenie repeated, jabbing a taloned finger into Frederick's chest for emphasis. "And a loser like you had to go and ruin it with *donuts*," he finished with palpable disgust.

"What's wrong with donuts?" Frederick knew it was a stupid question the minute it left his mouth but he was still so shocked by the transformation of the trick-or-treaters into very real monsters that he didn't really know what else to say.

"Nothing's *wrong* with donuts, Dude" the orange creature said, taking a bite out of his. "Not most of the time. But tonight is Halloween," he ended, as if expecting Frederick to immediately know what he was talking about.

"Chocolate," the littlest monster piped up in a high pitched voice.

"Let me explain something, Bro." The green one plopped itself into Frederick's favorite chair and propped its bare, taloned feet up on the coffee table. From its attitude, it was the ring leader.

"We get out one night a year. One." He paused meaningfully to let his statement register, but Frederick was still baffled. "You still don't get it, do you?"

"Gnarly, man," Orange said, looking at him pityingly. "Totally gnarly. Hey! I'm gonna check in the fridge to see if there's any brews. Want one?" He vanished down the hall.

"Take a load off..." the green creature closed its eyes for a second as if trying to remember something. "...Frederick!" it finally said, obviously pleased with itself.

"How did you know my...?"

"Have a seat, Freddy, because we may be here awhile."

Frederick sank onto the couch, his mind dull, not quite believing what was going on in his living room.

"I can see you don't know jack shit, do you buddy?" He sighed, apparently resolving himself to the burden of educating Frederick out of ignorance. "It's Halloween..."

"I know it's Halloween," Frederick cut in, a little testily.

"That's the spirit!" Greenie grinned. "Thought we were gonna lose you to shock there for a minute or two."

A huge belch, louder than a car engine revving, came

floating down the hall.

"I found the beer!" Orange called, redundantly. "You guys sure you don't want some?"

"Chocolate!" Purple Dotted wailed. "Chocolate!"

"Um...I think I have some cocoa in the pantry," Frederick told her, kindly. "Maybe I could go make some?"

In spite of the teeth, she was terribly cute and Frederick was afraid she'd start to cry if she didn't get her candy. Her glance of annoyed disdain at his suggestion of hot chocolate (and her fang-baring snarl!), quickly disabused him of any fears that her feelings could be so easily hurt.

"Some of us," Green continued as if he'd never been interrupted, "come for the booze. Oh! Not him. He'd drink soda if he had to. It's the burping he likes. Doesn't really care what causes it."

As if to punctuate Green's statement, another loud belch echoed from the kitchen.

"Chili," Purple added with a shudder.

"Yeah," Green frowned. "You gotta be careful of that. When he really gets going and it comes out the other end..." He shook his head and grimaced. "Anyways, some come up for the hubba-hubba, you know what I mean?"

He winked, an action which rather impressed Frederick as Green did not appear to have any actual eyelids, and moved his hips back and forth slightly. Frederick stared at him blankly.

"I can't...I don't understand."

"You know..." Green pumped his hips again. He sighed at Frederick's obtuseness and said, "Ex-say."

"Sex?"

"Dammit, Frederick!" Green shouted. "Not in front of the kid!"

"Sex?" The word came hesitantly from cute little lips which failed to hide a fang-filled smile of happiness at learning something new.

"Now see what you did?" Green was pissed. "Honestly, you people and your freaking potty mouths!"

"There's nothing dirty about…"

"Hey! Hey!" Green wagged a cautionary finger. "She's under age, you pervert. Watch it."

"Sorry," he mumbled.

"Where was I? Right." He settled back into the chair, and leaned forward when his own feet caught his attention. He reached down and plucked something from between his toes and, after examining it for a moment, popped it into his mouth and chewed lustily.

"Some come up for the *ex-say*. Others, usually those high-society types, raid the casinos or break into jewelry stores. I got a couple of friends who make the rounds of the drug dealers. Oh boy!" He chuckled. "They're gonna be impossible to deal with for the next few weeks, let me tel-lya! Others are more traditional. They go straight for the blood and guts. Of course, the true conservatives end up walking around with stacks of contracts looking for souls."

"Souls?" Frederick's head was spinning.

"Yeah, don't that just take the cake? It'd bore the crap outta me."

"The child…?" Frederick felt compelled to remind him.

"What? You mean…crap?" Green scoffed. "They're just words, Freddy my boy. Crap. Shit. Piss. Asshole. You see?"

"Sex!" Purple cried gleefully.

"Hey! Hey!" Green glared at her. "You watch your mouth, young lady. You hear?"

"Sex." She whispered the word this time, defiantly, but subsided into truculent silence when Green shot her another warning look.

A third belch split the air as Orange reentered the room and Green rolled his eyes. "You see what I got to work with?"

Green scratched his belly and seemed to feel something

under his shirt. He lifted it to examine his navel and, with a soft delighted cry of, "Gotcha!" he plucked something that was too small for Frederick to see. He placed it on his tongue, his eyes rolling up as if in ecstasy at the taste, and happily started munching.

"Technically, we're gluttons," Green continued, once he'd swallowed. "Mostly, we get all we want. But then, there's...chocolate."

"Chocolate..." Purple's eyes glazed and a dreamy look appeared on her face.

"Chocolate is divine," Orange told him solemnly. There was a strange percussive sound and the room was filled with an unbelievable putrid stench.

"Sorry," Orange seemed contrite. "I found half a pizza in the fridge. Garlic and anchovies."

"Like we couldn't tell," Green gasped, waving his hand in front of his face to drive away the fumes. "For the luvva all that's unholy, will you open a window?"

"It'll fade," Orange told him. "It always does."

Gagging, Frederick stumbled to the wall-mounted air conditioner. Even though it was a chilly night, he turned it on full blast. In moments, though the stench lingered, the air was breathable again.

"We don't get much chocolate," Green continued, once they were all settled again. "Lucky for us, on the one day we get up here, people are just giving it away." His broad smile slowly faded into a scowl. "And then some wise-ass like you offers us...*donuts*? I mean, come *on!*"

He sprang to his feet and continued talking, waving his arms and pacing back and forth in front of the fireplace, kicking Frederick's legs every time he passed.

"Some people just don't understand. I get that. I really do. We get jellybeans and caramels and licorice and those little sugar candies that are sort of like mints...except they aren't. Those are all very nice but we can get that stuff any time, ya know?"

Frederick didn't know, but he nodded just the same, not wanting to risk making any more waves.

"Hard candy though," Orange shuddered. "That's the worst."

"Oh no!" Green hastened to correct him. "Those fruit drops. The ones that *look* like chocolate M&Ms but they're not?"

"Skittles!" Purple said and made a gagging noise.

"There is a very special hell," Green intoned with great gravity, "for people who give out Skittles masquerading as chocolate M&Ms."

"Amen!" Orange and Purple said in unison.

"Thankfully, the days of handing out caramel apples and peanut butter crackers and candy cigarettes are over. Do you realize..."

He stopped in his tracks and fixed Frederick with a severe stare reminiscent of a high school teacher demanding a quiz answer from a recalcitrant student.

"Do you know the percentage of people who give out chocolate candy on Halloween has been increasing for the past couple of decades?" He nodded emphatically, as if Frederick was about to contradict him. "It's true. Yeah, yeah, yeah. I know. There's still stuff like malted milk balls and some of the tree-huggers have switched to the organic free range, free trade or whatever stuff. But you know what they say, right?"

"Er...no, I don't." Frederick was quite overwhelmed.

Not ten minutes ago he'd been headed for bed. Now, there were three demons in his house; one that talked a mile a minute, one that passed the most hellaciously pungent gas imaginable, and one that was, apparently, the under-aged child of whatever passed for the demonic equivalent of Puritan parents.

"Even bad chocolate," Green leered as if discussing

the attributes of the latest centerfold, "is better than no chocolate!"

All three chimed in, cackling at what seemed to be a familiar joke.

"So we look forward to this night all year long and..." His expression soured. "We get...donuts? What kind of a monster gives out donuts on Halloween?"

"I had a lot of candy earlier," Frederick protested, bristling at the insinuation that he was an insensitive candy disburser. "And it was almost all chocolate..."

"And that does us any good...how?" Green wanted to know.

"I ran out," Frederick finished, lamely.

Orange clucked his tongue and Purple once again wore that expression that would have indicated she was about to burst into tears—if she hadn't been gnashing her teeth so loudly.

"So what the *hell* are we supposed to do *now*?" Green roared.

"I don't know," Frederick said. "But there's little point keeping me prisoner because of it."

"Prisoner?" Unlike Green, Orange did in fact have eyelids and eyebrows, to boot. The latter rose to the middle of his forehead when his eyes widened with amusement. "You think you're a prisoner? Oh man, have you got it wrong, Dude. We just, like, need you to do us a favor, you know?"

"A favor?"

Green took control of the conversation again. "It's not like we can go out and get chocolate for ourselves now, is it?"

"I don't see why not."

Frederick thought his answer was quite a reasonable one. But the three creatures stared at him as if he'd suddenly grown two heads although, considering what *they* looked like, perhaps that was a lousy analogy.

"You're kidding again, right?"

Frederick shook his head, no.

"What the heck are we supposed to use for money, doofus?" Green yelled, waving his arms.

"Um...I didn't...I mean..." Frederick stammered.

"Oh, I get it." Green sneered down the length of his angular nose. "Thieves. You just assumed we were thieves, didn't you? You humans!" His disgust was even more palpable this time. "Judgmental pricks, aren't you?"

He stalked to stand in front of Frederick's chair and brought his face so close to Frederick's that the human could see every tiny blemish—which were a darker green, by the way, a lovely shade of emerald—and smell the hollow staleness of his breath.

"What kind of half-assed example are you setting for the kid here? Encouraging that kind of dishonesty? I already told you, we're all about the gluttony."

"If you want coveting," Orange added, helpfully, "you wanna keep an eye out for the guys with the long slinky hands and the black overcoats. Or maybe," he frowned with the effort of thinking, "...maybe that's lust. I get 'em mixed up."

"The grocery stores..."

Frederick was exceedingly uncomfortable with the demon's face so close to his own. He was uncertain whether the fellow had come so near because he was trying to drive home a point or because Green was going bite off his nose. In the latter case, he feared Green might devour it with as much gusto as he ate whatever unfortunate creatures lived between his toes and infested his belly button. Frederick could feel perspiration beading on his forehead and dampening his armpits. Even worse, he'd forgotten to take his acid reducers after dinner and the combination of the two Snickers Bites and the stress was making the acid churn in his stomach and start to burn its way up his esophagus.

"The grocery stores are closed at this hour," he finished, miserably, half certain that the statement would settle his fate to forevermore walk around both acidic *and* noseless.

"The grocery stores are..." Green's eyes narrowed to slits, glinting with a light that looked very dangerous from where Frederick was sitting so close.

"Well!" he exclaimed a moment later. His tone was far less angry and far more amused and rueful than Frederick had expected. "Closed. Ain't that a bitch? As usual, we get stuck with the fuzzy end of the lollipop stick."

"The melted part of the ice cream cone," Orange added mournfully.

"The crumbly corner of the donut box," Green said, casting a pointed glance Frederick's way.

Frederick shrugged, hoping the movement would be interpreted as sympathetic and, to his surprise, emitted a fairly large burp himself.

Orange's head jerked up from where he had been picking through the detritus of the fireplace and the dust bunnies under the couch and slurping up the more appetizing morsels he found there. He looked impressed.

"Good one, Dude!"

"Oh, excuse me!" Frederick blushed with embarrassment. "Acid reflux," he explained.

Green nodded, sympathetically. Given what Frederick had seen of the kinds of things his visitors put into their systems, he would not be at all surprised if all of them—human and...whatever, alike—had stomach ailments in common.

"Chocolate," Purple said.

This time, Frederick heard a new quality in her voice. He wasn't sure was it was exactly, but it held notes of happy anticipation, curiosity and something quite a bit darker.

"Chocolate," she repeated and her little button nose wrinkled as she sniffed the air.

Her companions snapped to attention, eagerly waiting for something.

Purple inhaled deeply and toddled over to stand next to Frederick's chair, her nostrils flaring in and out like they were attached to a bellows. She sniffed the air, smiled dreamily and incidentally exposing those sharp, silvery fangs to Frederick's great discomfort. His tongue flicked out, presumably to taste the air. Frederick saw it was forked like a viper's except for the fact that there were far too many forks in it for any self-respecting snake to fit into its mouth. He flinched when Purple leaned in even closer than Green had been and the many tendrils of her tongue gently caressed his face, eventually gathering as one and lingering in the vicinity of his lips.

Purple pulled back, gazing at him with a kind of triumphant satisfaction and announced, "Chocolate."

"Oh reeelly?" Green said, the picture of studied nonchalance. Then, his attitude changed and he leaned forward, and asked mockingly, "I thought we said we were fresh out of chocolate?"

"We did," Frederick was stammering again. "I mean...I was...I are...um...I am. I ate the last two pieces and..." He blushed again. "There must have been some on my breath when I...er...belched."

"Chocolate!" Purple demanded, either unable or unwilling to understand his explanation. "Chocolate!" she cried, louder this time, and her little body began to tremble and then to jiggle as if her skin had turned into polka-dotted Jell-O.

"Uh oh," Orange said, shaking his head sadly. "Now you've done it, dude."

Frederick looked at Green, helplessly. He had no idea what was going on but, if the cute little demon were about to have a seizure, he would have thought her guardians would rush to stop it.

"She doesn't believe you," Green explained. "She probably thinks you're hiding it somewhere."

"But..." Frederick protested.

Green shrugged. "I'd back off if I were you." As if to demonstrate, he scrambled to put the bulk of the couch between him and Purple.

Baffled, but unwilling to argue with the creature, Frederick rose from his chair and, shooting concerned glances over his shoulder at the distressed little monster, he moved toward the stairs. His concern lasted only until he put his foot on the first riser. Then, he froze in place, waiting for his brain to digest what his eyes were feeding it.

The pink and turquoise dots on the smallest demon's skin began to bubble as if being scalded from beneath. Each time a blister popped, the area beneath it seemed to expand so that, very shortly, she towered over the rest of them. The adorable little demon with the moderately disconcerting silver fangs had grown into a rather large and ominous demon with some seriously disturbing dentition.

"Chocolate!"

No longer charmingly high-pitched and childlike, her voice boomed stridently, so loud that Frederick's living room windows rattled in their frames.

"Chocolate!"

Her voice rose to a shriek that was louder than most fire alarms and Frederick got his hands over his ears before his eardrums shattered. The ceramic knick-knacks atop his fireplace mantle were less fortunate and shards littered the hearth.

"Chocolate!"

With the third outburst, Purple—now far more imposing than Frederick had ever imagined she could be—seized the couch, lifting it into the air, and did her best to tie it into a pretzel. She failed but, by that time, the couch was beyond caring. She tore through the wreckage, sniffing like a hound dog on the trail of a rabbit and, when she found nothing, she moved on to eviscerating Frederick's chair.

"Looks like she's on a roll," Orange commented mildly.

"You don't have a stash of chocolate hidden around here somewhere? You're sure?"

Frederick shook his head. "Just the cocoa powder in the kitchen."

"Pity," Green said, without making much of an attempt to fake any.

For the next several hours, Frederick watched in dismay while Purple rampaged through his house, searching for the illusive and non-existent chocolate. Fortunately for him, she wasn't actually violent, just destructive. She shoved him from her path when she found him obstructing her efforts to rip apart a mattress or pulverize a kitchen cabinet, but she did so absently. It wasn't as if she had any burning desire to harm him, but rather because she was so fixated on her goal that he'd better be wary of getting in her way. Even so, Frederick knew that for the next few months while he was arguing with his home owner's insurance claims agent, he was also likely to be recovering from bruised ribs, kicked shins and black and blue biceps and thighs.

Around three in the morning, Purple looked to be slowing down. But then she unearthed the stale partial remains of a Hershey's bar that Frederick had half-eaten and stuffed into a kitchen cabinet who-knew how many years ago, and she developed a second wind. To further fuel her frenzied quest, when she tore off the refrigerator door, she discovered an almost empty bottle of generic chocolate syrup and immediately guzzled the dregs, ignoring the outraged protests of her companions that she needed to share.

As dawn approached, Frederick's home was in a shambles. Every piece of upholstery had been disemboweled. The kitchen cabinets had not only been emptied, but also ripped from their mounts in case an elusive piece of chocolate might have been hiding behind them. Neither can, nor box, nor jar, nor canister had escaped being emptied. Even the contents of the trash compacter and recycling bins were fair game.

Upstairs, Frederick's clothes were in such a state that even the most desperate Goodwill store would have rejected them. Purple had tugged so hard on the dresser drawers that some of them had fallen completely apart. The contents of the rest were strewn about the room and down the hall. And in the spare bedroom that he used as a little office, the books, files and other personal stuff were fit only to be used as landfill. The shelves themselves, along with his antique roll top desk, were so much kindling.

As night faded and the sky started to lighten, Purple's search grew even more frantic. By the time dawn threatened the horizon, Frederick's three visitors gathered again in the living room. Purple slowly returned to her original size and tiny bright lemon-yellow tears of heartbreak made runnels down her once again cute little cheeks. Orange shuffled his feet back and forth, frustrated and disappointed, while Green cursed up a blue streak, albeit taking care to do it without mentioning the word sex.

When the sunlight streamed in through the broken living room windows and illuminated the wreckage that, only a scant few hours ago, had been the accumulated cherished possessions of his life, Frederick blinked back a few tears of his own. By the time he wiped his eyes with a torn shirtsleeve, the demons were gone, vanished back to wherever they'd come from for another year, if what they'd told him were true.

~

A year passed and the afternoon of the next Halloween saw Frederick at the third of the five supermarkets he was planning to visit. The stock people and baggers and other employees whispered amongst themselves, astounded. Never before in the history of the Goody Foods chain had any customer literally emptied the shelves to the extent that Frederick had done. The man had stuffed *nine* carts to overflowing with chocolate bars, chocolate covered pretzels and nuts, chocolate candies, fudge sauce and the store's entire stock of bottled chocolate syrup. The situation was even crazier when one of the cart boys from the parking lot reported that the customer was driving a full-sized van that was already crammed full of bags and cartons full of what looked like, from what he could see by peering in through the front windshield, even *more* chocolate!

The befuddled checker tallied the strange man's purchases and, just after the customer handed her his credit card, she noticed an item pushed to the side of the belt that she had forgotten to scan.

"Oh, I'm sorry, sir. Are these yours as well?" she asked, trying to be helpful.

The man looked at what she held in her hand and his face turned a very peculiar color. For a moment, she feared he was about to pass out or have a heart attack or some kind of stroke. His mouth moved as if he was trying to speak, but nothing came out except a hiss of air.

"No," he finally managed to croak out. "And please..." He looked like he was about to burst into tears or start screaming. "*Please*," he begged. "Get them *away* from me!"

Puzzled, she shrugged and put the item under the counter for one of the stock boys to return to the shelf later. No matter how strange or quirky he might be, Goody Foods' policy was that the customer was always right. Nevertheless, the cashier could not for the life of her figure out what had caused such a strong reaction in the chocolate-obsessed man.

After all, it was only a box of donuts.

THE HAIRY ONES

By Terry M. West

Red Hammond knew the consequences of chasing other gods. There was a law, a holy decree, which he was breaking. A sacrifice to the hairy ones was a blasphemous act. But he was committed to the demons in the woods by his very bloodline.

He had made peace with it long ago, but his wife, Nora, still fretted over it all. They had shared a home and life for nearly fifty years, but Nora still loathed this autumn ritual. She had been a Christian before her vow to Red. Nora had abandoned her faith to be with her husband. She had given up on her God and embraced the old ways.

Red and Nora's aged armchairs rested side by side. Red had a newspaper pulled up to his face. Nora bit her lip and stared at the front door. She waited anxiously for the night to end.

The boy started moaning again. Nora rose.

"You know you're not to go out there, woman," Red cautioned. His eyes stayed on the newspaper as he reached for his pipe.

Nora settled back against her chair and frowned. "And they shall no more offer their sacrifices unto evil spirits, after whom they have gone astray," Nora recited gravely.

Red put the paper aside. He took off his reading glasses and folded them into his breast pocket. "We do what must be done. We do what has been done for generations."

"The blood of it weighs on me," Nora confessed. "My faith weakens."

"I don't fault you none. But it is our path," Red told her.

Nora found more pain inside. Her gray face scowled. "You bring these lost children to me and I take to them, because I have none. You do this to me every year. You make me a mother for a month or so and then you tear them away and it breaks my heart, Red."

"I know, mama," Red said, taking his wife's hand. "Our crops grow undaunted and we do well. But a price hangs on these things."

The boy moaned louder. It was the only noise they could hear coming from outside. There was usually a chorus of coyotes at the river bed around this time of evening. This night, Halloween night, all was quiet and still out there. The hairy ones were coming, and the creatures of the forest hid cautiously.

Only Duncan, the homeless teenager Red had found in Weatherford, faced the darkness. He was naked and tied up on the porch, his arms and legs bound and spread between the wood columns that supported the porch roof. Red had engraved an ancient character onto the boy's chest. Duncan bled from the cut, but Red knew the wound would attract no animals. The boy was marked for the hairy ones.

Nora had adorned the porch with decaying Halloween decorations and freshly carved jack-o-lanterns; but the farm was set so far into the wild that only the forest spirits could appreciate the display. Red had never greeted trick-or-treaters at the door of the house. He didn't bother with holiday provisions. No one came to his step on Halloween; except the hairy ones.

"The boy was smart and so funny," Nora carried on. Her heartbroken eyes were still on the door. "*You* never get to know them. But I have to, Red. I have to make a home for them until the slaughter."

"We're kind to the pigs and the chickens as well, mama. But then butchery comes and we prosper. It is the way of things," Red explained, sucking on his pipe.

They could hear the howls of the hairy ones in the distance. Red turned off the reading lamp, darkening the living room. He smothered his pipe.

"They're coming," Nora whispered, clutching at her blouse.

"It's almost done," Red said, putting his hand on his wife's knee. He felt her tremble beneath his touch. "One last chore and then this is behind us for another year."

Nora closed her eyes and she shook. "The worst is yet to come. I hate it."

"Just let them do what they will, mama," Red urged. "It offends me as well, to be taken and to see you taken thusly. But it's a part of this, and it all washes off."

The hairy ones came closer. Red could sense them prowling nearby. Nora's hand tightened on his.

Duncan's swelling wails confirmed the arrival.

The hairy ones had the boy. Duncan's screams were rich with agony and terror and they rang through the thick gag that Red had placed across the boy's mouth. Red always gagged them. Otherwise, the children would make frightened pleas to Nora, and this was a torture that she couldn't endure.

The old couple sat in the darkness and clung to one another. They recited a dark and old prayer.

The screams subsided quickly. The torment never lasted that long. The hairy ones were too famished to be cruel.

Red waited for the flutes. They finally sang.

"It's time," Red said somberly.

The two disrobed quietly. They were comfortable with each other in their bareness; neither had a shy bone. Red looked at his wife's old flesh and he saw the flirtatious young girl who had trapped his heart years ago. He felt sad and dread tickled his stomach.

Red knew the orgy would be foul and long. The muddy violations upon the couple would be numerous. Their bodies would be dirtied and mined for pleasure until dawn. But it would appease the hairy ones; for a time, at least.

Red and Nora clutched hands and walked out into the night. They stood on the porch. The cold wind strengthened.

The boy was gone. The ropes that had held Duncan danced.

"Gratias agimus tibi propter liberalitatem," Red proclaimed to the dark. His body shuddered.

Faces crept into the glow of the jack-o-lanterns. The horned things were covered with fur and blood. Their smiles were wet and their black eyes shimmered with a horrible affection.

THE DEAL

By Janet Joyce Holden

Evan's consciousness was waiting. It was standing at the end of an alley partially obscured by fog, and reaching it was proving difficult while the threat of an intolerable headache blocked his path. But caution hovered in the murk, too. Like the prick of a dagger or a flame at his fingertips, and soon it became a matter of urgency to dash toward a state of awareness, and to hell with the pain.

His vision cleared, he lifted his throbbing head, and he saw he was lying on his back, naked and spread-eagled, secured by wrists and ankles to rusty metal rings fastened down to a hard wooden floor. Immediately he panicked and began to struggle, and despite the freezing temperature his limbs and torso were soon glistening with sweat. He craned his neck and searched his surroundings, and became aware of a small lantern hanging on a peg and beyond it, a room stinking of rot, its corners wrapped in depthless shadow where all manner of things could hide.

Dust fell from above, and for a horrible moment he wondered if the ceiling might fall on his head. A moment later a door opened, so close he felt the chilly dash of displaced air. Sweat turned to dread and soaked beneath his skin.

A familiar face arrived, accompanied by a second lantern. "So, you're awake."

"Joey?" Evan's anger flared. It poked his memory and

pushed aside some of the fear. "What the fuck is this?"

"You don't remember? You were back in town, and we got talking at the bar over on Ferris Street. Oh, and I put something in your drink. I apologize if it's given you a headache."

The bar. Ferris Street. He could barely remember. "Shit, Joey, let me loose." He looked beyond his right shoulder and along the length of his arm. The additional light offered no hasty cable ties, no duct tape. Instead the wrist had been carefully wrapped with thick hemp. The bindings were neat, the knots were reverently done, which probably meant he'd been out for a while. He pulled harder and winced. "C'mon, this isn't funny."

"Oh, I agree." The other man placed the lantern on the floor; he sat alongside it and got comfortable. "Do you know where we are?"

"How the hell should I?" *You spiked my beer, you prick.*

Joey shrugged. Still painfully thin after all these years: shoulders arched like the folded wings of a vulture, cheekbones sharp enough to cut glass. "We're in the Chase House. Remember how we were reminiscing about Hallowe'en all those years ago? About what you guys did to me? You and Terry?"

"I don't..." Evan tried to recall but it was difficult while his head was still pounding. He blinked, and stared at the ceiling. The stupid Chase House? In the midst of their old neighborhood, with its leaning walls, a rotten gate and an overgrown yard, Evan couldn't remember anyone ever living there. Rumors had whispered of the Depression era, and the disappearance of one family after another from within its confines. Although he'd heard his father laugh and say folks had simply skipped town to avoid the debt collectors. Nonetheless, throughout Evan's childhood the house had gained haunted status and its exploration had proved irresistible. It had also become host to one minor act of childhood cruelty that, by the looks of it, had come all the way around and was now biting him firmly in the ass.

He tried to stay calm. "That was years ago. We were just—"

"—kids? Yeah, I know. That's what Terry said, too."

Evan frowned. Terry. It had been Terry's idea from the start, but yeah—they'd both jammed the door so Joey couldn't get out, even though they knew their friend was scared witless and his dad would take his belt to him for being home late. That had been part of Terry's plan, too. A vindictive little bastard Terry was, who'd always made sure Evan was a full partner in his crimes. And it had never been the same after that night. Three friends had become two. And when Evan had gone to college, even that dubious partnership had dissolved.

He'd heard Terry had left town, had simply taken off in his beat up old car. No contact, no calls, no Facebook—nothing. Like he'd dropped off the face of the earth.

Evan swallowed. Regret arrived and danced with his fear, leaving his anger to wither. "Hey, look, I'm sorry. And if it means anything I came back for you and you'd already gone."

His captor nodded dispassionately. "I know, but it was too late by then. I trusted you, and you didn't stop him."

"Come on, man, I said I was sorry. You have to let me go. This is stupid. It's kidnapping."

Joey shook his head. He rose to his knees and stood up. "Not kidnapping—it's payment. I had to make a promise that night." He picked up both lanterns.

"What—are you just going to leave me here? I'll fucking freeze to death." And when Joey didn't answer. "Don't I even get a light?"

When the other man had closed the door, leaving him in absolute, utter darkness, he tried yelling. He screamed until his throat hurt. He tried shifting his body and moving his fingers but he couldn't get a grip on anything. Regret and fear left him alone. Terror paid him a call instead and gleefully suggested Joey had gone bat shit crazy and would set the house on fire with him in it.

But this was simply a prank, wasn't it? Long overdue, sure, but he'd be okay. He'd be fine, providing he didn't succumb to hypothermia.

In an attempt to stay calm, Evan kept on hauling on the ropes and he considered the whereabouts of his clothes, his phone and his car keys. All the while trying to forget he was tied to metal rings that looked way too old and permanent for this to be a spur of the moment prank.

But now dread was closing in, despite all his efforts to get free. He couldn't see himself, but he could imagine his pale glistening flesh, his pathetic shriveled genitals and his limbs all stretched out. His wrists hurt and his fingers were turning numb, and yet he thought he could feel the rope stretching a little. Maybe if he kept working on it.

He took a deep breath. Yeah, he'd just keep working on it and screw that sonofabitch.

~

Joey sat outside, on porch steps littered with fallen leaves, surrounded by a neighborhood the city had long since cast aside. He didn't want to stay and listen, but knew it was due penance. And when Evan began yelling, Joey's hands shook so hard it took him a few awkward attempts to turn off the lanterns.

Minutes later, when the screaming began again, this time with a greater urgency and at a higher pitch, Joey leaned forward, wrapped his arms around his knees and squeezed his eyes shut, and he didn't open them until the screaming stopped. He whimpered during the dull thumping sounds. He cried out as he heard a muffled, wet slap on the floorboards and he dug fingernails into his arms when he heard bones snapping like gunshot. There'd be nothing left, not a scrap. Not even the rope.

When it was done, when Evan had been utterly consumed, Joey stared absently into the dark and considered the cost. Payment. Two lives for the price of one. Brokered when those beneath had emerged from sleep inside this infernal house, where his so called friends had imprisoned him all those years ago on Hallowe'en. And while Terry's abduction and sacrifice had been easy, because he'd had it coming, it was an altogether different matter with Evan, despite the betrayal. And they had always insisted on his best friend, as part of the original agreement, even though he'd brought many others to the house over the years.

He stood up. He picked up the lanterns, walked down the path, and what remained of his humanity fell away like an old snakeskin. The street lay in darkness and ruin. The entire community lay derelict and forgotten. And now Evan was gone, that part of his life was forgotten too. Instead, he belonged to them; to those who had always lived *under*. Who were willing to allow the city to grow, providing it wasn't right here, and providing their needs were satisfied.

He crossed the street and climbed into Terry's old car, appropriated a long time ago. Just a couple of blocks and he'd arrive at smooth asphalt, streetlights and well-tended houses. Another year and the city would continue to thrive, and once more he'd be back, in order to appease his masters' hunger. This was how it was, how it always would be, and it was all part of the deal.

OUTLAWS OF HILL COUNTY

By John Palisano

The night before Halloween the Long Fellow sucked Jenny Lou Harrison's soul right through her fingers. Bright red strands connected her freshly blackened fingertips to his. She wiggled and cried. I just stood there by that big oak tree outside her room and watched, unable to do a damn thing to stop it from happening.

When he was done, he hurried out of her room, out her window and jumped into the crest of the tree above me. I hunkered down, scared it might see me and make me its next victim.

Instead, the Long Fellow bowed his head. He had a face with two large, gray eyes, a long nose and a mouth filled with small jagged fangs that reminded me of broken shards of glass.

All the acid in my stomach rose up. My balance went out, and I buckled down against the trunk, hugging that oak tree with the single ounce of energy I had.

His hot breath blanketed the back of my head and neck. My hands wiggled uncontrollably like the old men at Tully's Tavern who'd downed years of whiskey. Once I rolled onto the grass, my body gave out. My sick hit the dirt. The smell of my own cooked bile made my guts clench.

The Long Fellow climbed the oak tree. Branches moaned and leaves rustled. Several twigs dropped near me. I wanted to get a better look at the Long Fellow—see what kind of creature could turn someone sick with its own will—see how such a thing drained the life from poor, pretty Jenny using only its unholy fingertips.

Harvest Hill felt colder that night than any other night I remember, even though it wasn't yet winter. Part of me believed the Long Fellow sucked every ounce of warmth and comfort from the air along with what he stole from Jenny Lou.

My throat felt dry and sore. The few inches I managed to raise myself up made my head spin.

Jenny Lou faded away.

~

I woke late that night. Something deep down inside me didn't want to believe the Long Fellow had returned to Harvest Hill. Hurrying from her house, I did my best to tuck my hair under my leather jacket's collar to try and keep a little warmer. One the benefits of having long hair, I guess. That, and everyone seemed to know where I stood concerning the war. Never thought going to Nam was a good idea. We have enough trouble at home.

Jenny Lou and I went out a few times, but always with a group, never just her and me. I would have loved to, of course, and was working up the courage to ask her. That was before the Long Fellow came and took away any chance of that happening.

~

Once I was in bed I couldn't sleep. My mind raced with images of the Long Fellow. No one would believe me. The Long Fellow was something the kids sang about—he wasn't real.

"When the night gets long

And the day goes quick,
You better hide inside,
Or you might get sick,
Out come the Long Fellow,
Playing his tricks,
Sucking your soul,
Through your fingertips..."

All of us knew the rhyme. We grew up singing the song and scaring each other with Long Fellow stories. Legend was he came down from the mountains on Halloween every year to feed on kids. He'd put out his hands and pull your essence from your fingertips, leaving them black and shriveled.

What was I supposed to do? I knew what I'd seen, but no one was going to believe me. Keep your mouth shut and forget it, I thought It wasn't real.

I raised my head and body on the pillow. My stomach felt better being elevated. It wasn't as comfortable as being all curled up, but eventually sleep found me.

~

"We've got some bad news this morning." That was how Mr. Palace started homeroom. Before the bell rang, I spotted him chatting with Mr. Block, our science teacher. Something about the way they stood with their backs to us made me believe they were sharing secrets.

"Probably canceling Halloween tonight 'cuz they think you dumb hippies are going to go and protest it," said Eric, a nasty piece of work who never had a good word about anything.

I just shook my head.

"Kids?" Mr. Palace said. "You're all old enough to hear the truth."

Get on with it, I thought. Come on.

"We lost Jenny Lou Harrison last night." His voice broke saying her name; he lowered his chin and put a thumb to his forehead before looking up.

My chest felt numb. How could she be dead?

The Long Fellow wasn't supposed to kill. He just left kids an empty, soulless shell. I thought: *I was there last night. Did anyone see me? Are they going to make the connection and pin me at her house? Are they going to arrest me? What am I going to tell them? That the Long Fellow did it?* I felt dizzy. Clutching the sides of my desk, I took a long deep breath.

"She passed away in her sleep. No one's sure exactly why, but we'll let you know as soon as we find out anything." Mr. Palace stood straight and put his hands on his hips like a drill sergeant.

Eric raised his hand. "I have a question."

"Shoot."

"Does this mean we're going to have to cancel Halloween after all?"

~

By the time third period rolled around, I knew I had to sneak out of Harvest High. "I think Steve Woodworth got a visit from the Long Fellow, too." My good friend Jules Shepherd bent my ear while we were switching books at our lockers. "He's got the same black fingers you were telling me Jenny Lou had. I saw him leaning on Mr. Strabb and going inside." He showed me his fingers. "I wonder if the Long Fellow gets me how anyone would know. My fingers are already black."

I smiled. Jules always tried to make light of things.

"This is too messed up. Kids are getting sick. Dying. We've got to cruise down to the nurse's office," I said

Jules wiggled his nose just a bit. It was a habit he had ever since I knew him. When he was scared or excited he tended to punctuate his sentences with a little twitch. "We got to play sick."

~

"You look just fine to me, Darling," Nurse Lorraine said, and was right. Even standing still, Jules looked like he just might pounce. He didn't look sick at all. Plus he was grinning ear to ear. "But I guess if you want to put your head down, it won't hurt. Just in case."

Jules stuttered. "Okay. Great. Good idea. I am dizzy now that you mention it."

She forced a grin. "Last room on the right," she said before looking at me. "And you, Mr. Garner: you look pale as a ghost. What's going on?"

"My stomach," I said. "Been killing me since last night." I placed my hand on my gut. I didn't have to imagine too hard.

"Last night?" she said. "That so?"

I nodded. "Yup. Just about nine o'clock."

She reached up and adjusted her green cube-shaped hat. It looked kind of like a military hat worn on the front lines. "Huh," she said. "Not cool."

We all had reason to believe Nurse Lorraine lived two lives: one where she took care of us kids at the school and the other where she got really into her Mary Jane and Dead records. Maybe it was because she wasn't much older than us.

"I don't think I'm really too sick," I said. "But I just thought I should get checked out in case."

"You look a little green around the gills. Why don't we get you lying down?"

I agreed.

Nurse Lorraine stood up. "Come on," she said. "Before you pass out." She smiled but didn't look me in the eye.

The rear of the nurse's office had several small open

rooms, each with its own cot. As we neared the back, I could see Steve Woodworth lying on a cot, his hands by his sides. I slowed down and saw his fingers, black and shriveled. "Jesus," I said.

"Keep going," she said. "Don't look."

"Why?" I asked. "What happened?"

Steven had the same affliction as Jenny Lou.

Nurse Lorraine said: "Put this under your tongue." She nodded and bent down a bit. As she did, a sliver of tie-die poked from between the buttons of her nurse's shirt. Nurse Lorraine was cool after all. She was one of us. She suddenly looked a lot prettier to me. Funny.

"Okay, so keep that there for five minutes. I'll be back to check on you." She nodded and I gave her a thumbs-up. I watched her walk out of my room and did not blink once. I couldn't help but see her differently. Suddenly, her straight, long blond hair and thin body made sense. She didn't have her hair up in a bun. She didn't wear a ton of make-up. She didn't look like my mom or any of our regular teachers who all looked stuck in *Leave It To Beaver*. Nah. Nurse Lorraine was a hippie. Peace and Love. I dug her.

I put my hands behind my head and closed my eyes. Long Fellow I had evidence right in front of me. But who would believe me? Who could I go to for help? None of the adults were likely to believe me.

Someone charged through the front door of the nurse's office. "We've got another one, Lorraine." It'd been Mr. Strabb talking. "Something bad's going on here. I think we need to call the Capitol or the State Department or someone in the District. I don't know."

Her chair squeaked on the tile as she stood. "Jeff? What happened?"

"Not sure," he said. "I don't feel so hot."

I took the thermometer out, read it, and leaned up on my elbows. I was just over 99 degrees.

"Hey?" It was Jules. "Let's go." he said. "I think we've seen enough here. Don't you?"

"I didn't even hear you get up," I said. "What're you doing?" He looked toward the Nurse's receiving area just as we both heard Jeff Scranton. "It hurts," he yelled. "Oh, God. Help."

Jules shrunk back inside my room.

"My fingers. I can't move my fingers," Jeff screamed.

"Calm down, Jeff. We'll figure out..."

"No. I need to go to the hospital. We need to call the police. The Long Fellow did this."

Mr. Strabb's voice turned stern and deep. "You've been reading too much Famous Monsters, mister."

"It's not that," he said. "It's real."

Their footsteps became louder. Jules looked to me. "We've got to sneak out," he said, whispering. "Soon as their backs are to us we have to run."

"Okay," I said, putting the thermometer back in my mouth and lying back down. Jules curved around the corner and out of view.

He looked at me for a moment and I shut my eyes. Then I heard them hurry past. "Oh, God, Miss Minerva, it really hurts," Jeff moaned. "Are you going to bring me to the hospital?"

"We'll do everything we can."

They passed and I opened my eyes. Jules waved. "Come on," he said. "Quick." We hustled out of there.

As we made it to the main room I heard Nurse Lorraine. "Lew? Where are you going? Do you have a fever?"

The door was closed and we were around the corner by the time she called again.

~

"We're going to Rob Cash's place?" Jules didn't sound excited. Then again, most folks weren't too thrilled with my cousin. He ran our small town biker gang, The Outlaws of Hill County.

"He'll know what to do," I said. "He's used to dealing with things outside the law."

Jules tugged at my sleeve. "This is outside everything. What makes you think he's going to believe us that the Long Fellow's here?"

"He'll believe me," I said. "I've never lied to him."

"People lie all the time." We "Asking someone to believe there's a monster in their town is a little hard to do, isn't it?" made it a little ways down Telegraph Hill.

I nodded. "Sure is," I said. "But *you* believe the Long Fellow's here, don't you? You ain't seen him in person."

We stopped and our eyes met.

"*You* saw the Long Fellow?"

"I'm going to wait and tell you and Rob what I saw at the same time," I said. "You still want in? Or do you want to go home and not help out?"

"It's Halloween?"

"So no one's going to think twice about why we're outside late hours. Who else do we have on our side? If Rob says he's not going to help then it'll be just us two. Not sure that's going to do the trick."

~

We rode our bikes down to Rob's place and found him relaxing on his porch with a beer and his Martin acoustic. "That's one sorry looking excuse for a Halloween costume," Rob said. "I can't believe you're even related to me." He pointed toward my head. "Who's going to believe a black kid and his Hippie friend with long hair who's wearing Army clothes?"

"You?" I said.

Rob took a big sip from his Moosehead before resuming picking at his Martin.

"Your hair's long," I said. "And you wear black leather jackets like all the greasers used to in the 50s."

"They were riders, too. Just like me. There's a relationship." He winked. "There's no connection between G.I. Joe and Haight, friend."

I pointed to the peace symbol I'd painted on the breast of the jacket. "Look," I said. "Peace. Love. I'm wearing this as a protest. I can be an Outlaw, too."

"Not really," he said. "You just look confused to me which side you're on."

"I'm a Hippie. I don't believe in war. I ain't going."

"You're sixteen. The war will be over by the time you're old enough to get drafted. It's going to be the 70s in a few months."

Jules said, "We've got to be out of Nam soon, right?"

"Hope so," I said. "And, yeah, talking about that, we need to talk about what's going on it town."

"I seen some real messed up shit," Jules said. "The Long Fellow's back."

Taking a moment to register what he'd just heard, Rob just said, "really?" and then kept strumming. It sounded a lot like something Richie Havens might play.

"I seen him last night," I said. "Outside Jenny Lou Harrison's house, Rob. I saw that thing sucking the life right out of her. And when he was through with her he climbed the tree over my head and I could smell his breath. Worse thing I ever smelled. Made my stomach hurt awful."

He stopped playing and looked up so that our eyes met. "You shitting me?"

"That thing's come back because it's Halloween," I said. "Knows it'll blend in."

"Her fingers looked like she had frostbite on the ends?" Rob asked.

I nodded. "Yup. That's right. Steve Woodworth came in to the Nurse's Office with the same thing. Then Jeff Scranton."

"I don't know," Rob said. "Sounds suspicious."

Jules and I looked at each other. Rob was supposed to believe us.

"Isn't that the same thing that happened with Dave?" I said.

Rob looked at me, then Jules. I knew I shouldn't have mentioned his brother, but I was desperate.

Jules shrugged. "Who's Dave?"

Rob charged Jules, grabbed his collar, and snarled. "That thing took him seven years back," he said. "That thing has come knocking around again looking for me now." Rob turned to me. "Is that what you're trying to pull?"

"Hell no," I said. "Not like that." My cousin, Rob's brother, had gone missing under mysterious circumstances. Rob claimed that some fellow with real long, claw-like hands came down and rooted his brother right up from the ground. Claimed there was a way the guy sucked the life out of his brother, leaving him for dead. Rob was the one who had to take the hit on it. His story could never be verified. Judge Robbins gave him involuntary manslaughter for five years. Said they'd probably both been drinking too much and probably Rob had egged him over the edge. I didn't buy it, but the law's the law. Like Creedence sings: you fight the law; they're going to win every time.

"You kids are fucking with me," he said. "I ain't got time for this."

"The Long Fellow's here," I said. "We've got to stop it."

Rob kick-started his gold Harley Davidson motorcycle. The cylinders purred; the engine vibrated. He reached inside his jacket, pulled out a Zippo, and lit up a Camel. Rob squeezed the clutch on the handlebar and rolled the gas with the other. On the shoulder of Rob's leather jacket, I spotted his hand-sewed gold 'Outlaws' patch. "Don't ever bring this up to me again," he hollered as he rode off, giving us the finger over his shoulder.

~

As we rode our bikes through town we realized Harvest Hill was deserted "Everyone's missing," Jules said.

"Everyone's getting ready for the Halloween assembly at the school," I said. "They're setting it all up right now, I bet. It's already getting dark."

"So we have to go back there?"

"Unless you've got a better idea."

~

As me and Jules pulled inside the Harvest Hill High parking lot, none of the lights were on and all the doors were locked. We leaned the bikes against a light post and went to the front of the school.

"Looks like trouble." Jules peered into the lobby through the glass doors by cupping his hands against the glass. "This makes no sense."

Grabbing his arm, I pulled him from the window. "I'm saying I'm agreeing with you."

We both craned our heads, trying to see who it could be.

"Hello?" I asked.

Sounded like someone walking on top of the school.

His eyes went wild. "Be quiet," he said before he looked me up and down. "What kind of Outlaw you going to make, anyway?"

Not knowing how to act or what to say, I backed away from the doorway.

We both heard skittering again.

Something thumped behind us, like someone had jumped off the roof and onto the sidewalk.

Standing between the parking lot, and us, a large silhouetted figure pointed at me. The sun was in back of him, so neither of us got a good look.

"Hey, man. We don't want any trouble." Jules stood

behind me. "We're just looking for our kin."

I squinted and tried making out the fellow's face.

The large figure pointed his finger toward Jules and hissed.

My eyes got used to the light. The thing the fellow gestured with was not a finger at all. It looked much more like a sickle-shaped claw.

The Long Fellow hissed again.

Jules pushed past and stood between the Long Fellow and me. "I know, I know," he said. "I see him."

"H-him?"

The Long Fellow jutted forward, bending at the middle. Opening its jaw, I imagined the thing must have been eating rocks to sport so many busted teeth. Some were black and sharp, like edges of broken bottles. A rancid smell like gasoline and spoiled seafood overtook us. The Long Fellow's breath was poison.

My eyes filled with water and my guts went all tight.

The Long Fellow let out an ungodly sound, which I heard through a daze, like he was on TV in another room.

I hurled on the sidewalk, turning away from Jules. *Keep yourself standing unless you want that thing to get you.*

From the corner of my eye I spotted Jules huddled on the ground. He'd had his own sick and wasn't moving. My head spun: I'd never felt so dizzy in all my life. I wanted more than anything to fall down and sleep.

Another blast of poison spewed from the Long Fellow's mouth. I tried to turn to see the thing, but the pain was too strong.

I retched again, only this time nothing came out besides a string of sticky spittle. It hurt worse than anything.

What's this thing want?

It should have been eating Jules, or at least taking him away. It should have used its sickle-arm to cut him.

It's probably already eaten half the town.

The Long Fellow spat another blast of poison, missing me. It leapt onto the roof and vanished.

"Jules?" My best friend was lying a few feet away. I stared at his rib cage: it was moving. He grunted. "We've got to go."

~

Inside the school, the halls were dark. Paper jack o' lanterns and scarecrows stared down from the walls. We'd made them to decorate for our Halloween assembly. I leaned my forehead against one of the cold, small rectangular classroom windows. The lights were off. A desk was overturned near the front of the room and appeared covered with thick, dark fluid. Small bits of what appeared to be chewed-up food dotted the floor.

"Someone attacked us." Jules rubbed his head and moaned. "Hit me over the head."

"The Long Fellow," I said. "Come here to fight."

"Yeah, well, my stomach hurts worse than anything. I'm in no condition to fight."

"Mine, too." I reached out my hand. "But we've got to do something."

From the other end of the hall someone threw up. It came from just outside the doors, on the back patio where some of the students hung out between periods.

Something smelled fishy and rancid. We crept toward the back door. He wasn't sure who was out there.

Whoever it was made another heaving sound, which was quickly followed with a nasty, large splatter-like thump on the concrete. We could hear him sighing and gasping.

Jules made his way to the far side of the hallway and signaled for me to follow. As we neared the end of the corridor we spied Eric Sable hunched over just outside the back door. A bright red trail of spittle wavered in the air from Eric's lips toward the ground.

Blood. More blood.

More vomiting followed. Eric put an arm out against one of the posts and retched.

Backing out from the rear hallway, we walked away as quickly as possible.

We made it to the gym, where music played inside. As soon as we were through the doors we knew where everyone had gone: to the Harvest High gymnasium for our annual Halloween show. In one corner there was a large tin bucket filled with water and apples. Miss Deloitte was watching the kids try their luck bobbing. To her right there were several small clusters of kids and students mingling and talking. Most importantly, to me, at least, was seeing The Amphibians jamming there right on the floor. Acid rock filled my gym. That was cool. Nurse Lorraine was stage left, nodding her head, sipping something from a straw.

"Quite the party," Jules said. "So what're we going to do?"

We wouldn't be waiting long for our answer. I heard the back door open and saw the Long Fellow walk inside. For a few brief moments no one but Jules and me even noticed.

"Nice costume," someone said.

The Long Fellow lowered his bony head and smiled.

Everyone around him scattered.

With one graceful leap, the Long Fellow made it to the center of the gym. It stared right at us.

"Holy shit, man," I said.

It hopped again, this time landing ten short feet from us. My eyes locked with the creature. My stomach hurt again, just as bad as it had the first time. My arm rose like someone had it on a string. My fingers spread out. So did the Long Fellow's. I noticed that the veins on top of his gray hands pulsed.

He squeezed his fingers as though he were milking an orange.

Blood rushed toward my fingers and pooled. I couldn't move a muscle. I couldn't even take my eyes off the Long Fellow, no matter how hard I tried.

"No," Jules said. "Not again."

The crowd hurried toward the rear gym door. Something pushed them back. Something loud. Something scared them backward. As the crowd spread themselves away from the door a half-ton Harley Davidson rolled right through them. The Outlaws. There's something in the pitch of those engines that sounded just perfect. I don't think I ever loved hearing that sound more than I did that Halloween. I couldn't help, though, but wonder where they heard the Long Fellow had come, or how. I imagined Rob must have signaled them somehow; he'd left them some kind of message.

As the first of the Outlaws rolled in to the gym, spreading the crowd against the walls, the second bike drove inside. It was Rob.

I still couldn't move. My fingertips were turning dark and my stomach wrenched on itself. Any second, I felt like I might fall down.

The band was still playing. Jules was nowhere to be seen. It seemed I was alone, standing inches from the Long Fellow while he drew my life from my hands.

Rob's Harley roared. The bike raced toward us; Rob was hunched down low toward the handlebars, his teeth gritted, his mouth snarling.

The Long Fellow turned in time to see the front wheel lift from the gym floor. The Harley was up on its back wheel. How the hell is Rob strong enough to pull a wheelie on a Harley? I thought. Those bikes weigh half-a-ton.

But he had, and impossible as it seems, the Harley drove full speed toward the Long Fellow. In a flash, the front wheel bashed into the Long Fellow's chest, sending the creature backward dozens of feet, breaking its connection to me.

Two more Harleys raced right behind Rob just as I fell to my knees. Once the connection to the Long Fellow was gone, what little energy I had left wasn't enough to keep me up. My hand tingled like it'd fallen asleep. I tucked it into my shirt without looking at it. I didn't want to know the damage. Not yet.

On the other side of the gym near the band, Rob circled the Long Fellow was on the ground and Rob was circling behind it.

The crowd screamed and gasped. Some of the band members were watching. I guess it was impossible not to notice.

The Outlaw with the red hair drove up near the Long Fellow and swung a massive metal chain around his head. His bike bucked; he lost his balance for a second because he was riding with one hand.

The Long Fellow jerked toward him, its mouth open, its sickle-shaped claws swung. Red flinched, but didn't stop rotating the chain over his head. It was getting faster and faster. On the opposite side of Red, I saw Rob doing the same thing.

Red whipped the chain at the Long Fellow and it wrapped around the creature's middle. Then Rob threw his chain, which made it round its neck.

Screaming and protesting, the Long Fellow threw out its arms. The chains fell off and you could see a big black mark across its chest where Rob's tire had struck. I saw little small splotches of blood throughout seep from the wound.

That thing bleeds red just like me, I thought. *Isn't that funny?* By then I was curled up on the gym floor watching the whole thing sideways.

Red bent down to pick up his chain and the Long Fellow swung. Red dropped and rolled onto his back. It looked like he'd fallen off his bike before and knew how to fall without hurting himself too bad. The Long Fellow swooped down and hit him again with its sickle-claw, slashing Red in the back. His leather jacket split. He stood up, although he was limping a little bit.

The Long Fellow made to strike again, but Rob managed to hoop his metal chain around its neck again. That gave Red time to hop back on his bike and twirl his own metal chain. The third Outlaw, one I never seen before, got chains around the Long Fellow, too.

Toward the back of the gym we spotted several more Outlaws watching the scene, although they seemed to be keeping folks out of the way more than anything.

When I turned around Red was nodding at Rob and the Long Fellow was wiggling like a stuck pig. It tried to jump and Rob jerked upward a little. He pulled his chain tight so that the Long Fellow couldn't raise itself more than a few inches. Red did the same. They nodded and Rob put both feet up and steered for the back door.

The Outlaws guarding the gym raised their arms to keep people back as Rob and Red dragged the Long Fellow across the way. At one point it dug its claws into the varnished wood flooring, scratching long ruts in its wake. It hollered, as if struck, but it was one of its black toenails that'd caught in the ruts. The Outlaws pulled the Long Fellow, breaking the nail off in the process. As soon as it'd passed, I spotted Jules run toward the nail, wiggle it free, and put it in his pocket.

The Amphibians kept right on playing. I don't believe they missed a single psychedelic note.

"Hey, there?" Nurse Lorraine bent over me, her eyes darting left and right real quick, scanning me.

I showed her my hand, careful to keep my eyes on her

and not look at it. "It got me a little," I said. "Hurts."

I held my wrist so that she could see. "We need to get you out of here," she said. "Are you cool otherwise?"

Wobbly on my feet, and doing my best to get up, I said, "I'm cool." She held me by the crook of my arm.

Before she walked me out of the gym, and away from the music, and the scattered crowd, we watched the Long Fellow screech and claw at its chains as the Outlaws rode into the night. I hoped they took the damn thing somewhere far away, and I hoped I never had to see it again, and I hoped they made it pay for Jenny Lou, and for me and my hand, and for everything it'd done to Harvest Hill.

Just outside the gym Jules caught up with me. "So wasn't Rob the guy who gave us the finger earlier?"

"Yup," I said. "Guess he had a change of heart."

"Can't believe that thing's real," he said and produced the nail for me to see. "At least I'll have this to remind me." He put it away.

I showed him my dark fingers. "And I've got these," I said. "Hopefully we're done with that thing forever."

Once we walked away none of us ever spoke of the Long Fellow again.

~

"Is that true?" Lew, Jr. asked his father.

His dad smiled and stood from his recliner. "Well we all grew up and the world replaced the Long Fellow with Vietnam, Communists and atom bombs. Heck: getting married and getting a 9-to-5'er seems more frightening." He winked at Lorraine, who'd brought them some cocoa. "But it is Halloween, after all. Never saw what happened to the Long Fellow. Rob never told me. If it's still out there somewhere he might decide he's hungry enough to come on down here again." He stretched his arms. Both his sons' eyes went immediately to their father's left fingers, which were a shade darker and covered with scar tissue.

"You even have the marks still?" Lew, Jr. poked his brother. "It is true. Poppa wouldn't lie to us."

When they turned their parents had gone, leaving them to look out their living room window, out toward their yard, their town, the big oak tree swaying in the wind, and the moon that hung low on the horizon. There was a scratching sound somewhere close by, followed by a faint howl. Then they could both swear they heard children singing outside, their voices carried on the cold October wind.

"When the night gets long
And the day goes quick,
You better hide inside,
Or you might get sick,
Out come the Long Fellow,
Playing his tricks,
Sucking your soul,
Through your fingertips..."

THE CROSS I BEAR

By David Winnick

Light filled the dome made by her sheets as the flashlight rolled in her lap. She could not stop the shivering which had overtaken her body. She flipped through the pages of her *Bible*, its gilded edges so sharp she could feel them wanting to slice through the tender tips of her fingers. She was unable to find the passages which would bring her solace. Every year, it was the same. Last night was spent preparing; she had gathered all of her things to protect herself from the monsters and demons which were out tonight wandering the streets. Momma and Daddy had warned her about them. This was the Devil's night and she was not to go out.

Dinner had been early. Top Ramen with scrambled eggs. It was her favorite meal and her parents did everything they could to make her happy. Occasional knocks on the door and rings of the bell had interrupted them during dinner. Each one had made her jump; her skin had crawled with the knowledge of who was on the other side. Old Scratch, the Devil himself was trying to tempt them. Open the door, he was saying. Let me in. He laughed from the other side, a high pitched cackle. He had brought other monsters with him and she could tell that they were enjoying their night.

After eating, her parents allowed her to watch one episode of *Davey and Goliath* before they sent her off to brush her teeth and go to bed. It was verging on six o'clock by the time she had shut her bedroom door, nearly two and a half hours before her normal bed time. She hated this night every year. She never slept. Instead she sat in her bedroom cowering and praying to the Lord that she would make it through the darkness.

The evening started with attempts at homework but those were no good. Momma knew how much this night scared her and would forgive her for not having tomorrow's work ready. She would get extra time to do it tomorrow. Momma was kind that way. She was the best, smartest teacher in the world. There was no one better. Who else knew about the dinosaurs being fake or that global warming was a liberal plot. Momma and Daddy knew everything.

At seven o'clock, she locked her door. She was safe inside. The front door would keep the monsters out. They couldn't come in unless you let them in. She knew it for a fact. For years the monsters had tried to get to her family with a constant barrage of tempting and baiting, every day they tried to destroy her family but it was always worse on this night. She knew that Momma and Daddy would keep her safe from the monsters at their door. Many nights she could hear them making their incantations and warding off the demons. Even now, she could hear Momma's voice echoing through the halls, holding them at bay.

"Don't! Stop!" she screamed, commanding the monsters to cease their ingress. The vehemence of her voice reminding Annie that her mother was the most powerful woman in the world.

Then Daddy, his voice strong and deep, helping to bolster Momma's words shouted, "Jesus, Yes! Yes, God. I want you to come. Come for me. Come for me."

Sometimes the prayers would work the first time, but every now and then, Momma and Daddy would have to try a second time. Sometimes it would take only a couple of minutes to expel the demons but other times, it would take what seemed like an eternity.

Annie had once asked if she could help them with their prayers, if there was anything she could do. They had smiled at her and said, "No." The only way that she could help them was to stay in her room and not disturb them. She knew that she was not yet strong enough to help. Her faith in the Lord was unwavering, but sometimes she would sin. It was not her fault. The Devil, it was his fault that she had sinned.

One time, she had taken two pieces of candy from a bowl at a restaurant instead of just one. She knew she shouldn't have done it but they were her favorite: small butterscotch disks. She had told no one and was so embarrassed by what she had done that she had thrown both pieces in the garbage the second she got home. Another time she had said a four letter word she heard on TV. Momma had been so mad; she had taken Annie into the bathroom and made her take a bite out of a bar of soap. That night, Annie sat up until dawn feeling like she was going to vomit. Momma had been right to do it.

No, she was not yet strong enough to help them. But on those nights, when Momma and Daddy were wrapped up in prayer, she would join in under her breath. "God, come for me, Jesus come, come for me and take me from this world, so full of evil." For when the rapture was at hand, she knew her parents would make it beyond this mortal plane and into the loving embrace of the Lord in Heaven.

The doorbell rang and she almost dropped her *Bible*. The lights had been dark in the house for hours. That was how you hid from the demons. The lights drew them. Even with the lights out, some still came to the door, asking for entrance. Only the biggest and the strongest would come to a place where they were not invited, a place where the power of God was so strong.

Again the bell rang. This time she expected it. She placed her bible down on the mattress and grasped the cross around her neck. Most nights, she would take it off and hang it on her bedpost. She knew it was not safe to sleep with a chain around her neck. The gold plated metal was cool in her hand. The edges of the charm cut into her palm, making small holes. Blood began to drip from the edge of her hand and onto the bed, soaking into the white cotton sheets.

An insistent knocking followed the bell. The Devil was trying to beat down the door. He would not accomplish it. All night he would try, over and over again, but he would not succeed in his evil work. Pounding and pounding, then his voice, much higher pitched and more youthful than she had imagined. "We know you are in there," it screamed. "Open up, trick or treat." The pounding stopped. Momma and Daddy's spell had worked. Jesus must have come and ushered the Devil away. Yes, that was it.

Annie turned back to her *Bible* reading the words of Paul. Daddy had told her time and time again that Paul was the wisest of all of the men in the *Bible*. He knew the truth of the world. She read the words of Paul again. "A man is the image and glory of God; but the woman is the glory of man." She knew that daddy loved her because she was his, his creation. The proof of his love for her was her existence. He was kind to her and to Momma. It was from Paul that he learned to treat them kindly, "Husbands, in the same way be considerate as you live with your wives and treat them with respect as the weaker partner." She wished to one day find a husband as kind as Daddy, a husband who had learned well the teachings of Paul.

Again, the doorbell rang. He was being more persistent than usual this year. She prayed for him to go away, to leave them alone. It was only one night every year but every year it got harder and harder. The Devil and his minions became more and more unyielding in their mockery. Their childish laughing was almost too much to bear. Her heart raced, and her hands trembled. She would never be strong enough. Never strong enough to defeat Lucifer.

But what had she learned from the teachings? Had she learned nothing? What did it say of her? So weak was she that each year she spent the entirety of October thirty-first cowering, hiding from the darkness outside the walls of her home. Momma and Daddy were not cowards. They spent the night fighting his evil with their prayers for Jesus to come. She was not a child anymore. She was becoming a woman now. Just two months ago, she had stained the bed sheets with blood for the first time. Momma had told her what it meant. She was getting older and she would soon be feeling the pull of the Devil more and more. Men were going to start looking at her in different ways. The Devil was inside them too.

How could she hide from his ways when he was all around them? She must learn, somehow to withstand the power. She must face the evil head on. That was the only way. The stories of David and Goliath, Joshua and the walls of Jericho. Did not Gideon defeat the Midian army with only a handful of men and his wits? These were not the stories of cowards like her. These were men of action, men who faced their enemy no matter what the odds. They did not fear death, for their faith in God was all they needed.

She closed her *Bible* and placed it on the bed. With sweaty palms, she pulled the sheets from over her head. Her room was dark and something cast shadows across the balcony curtains. They danced in the pale light emanating from the street lamps, the shadows of the monsters. Annie ground her teeth as she placed her feet on the floor. The soft carpeting squished between her toes. With careful steps, she made her way across the room. She must be quiet. It would not do to disturb Momma and Daddy when they were working so hard to bring Jesus to them. No, they would not like to be disturbed. She was supposed to be asleep. She made her way to the balcony doors. Slowly, she wrapped her index finger around the red curtains which separated her from the evil outside. She must be strong, she told herself. Carefully, she pulled the curtain to the side, just enough to peek out. Annie leaned into the small gap, her eyes searching across the cul-de-sac.

It was worse than she could have possibly imagined.

The neighborhood had erupted into an orgy of evil. Truly, Hell had taken over outside. Monsters and imps roamed the street, their faces marred with the dark evil they had taken into themselves. Swarms of them wandered about, skipping and laughing as they moved from home to home. They carried bags and buckets for collecting their tithings. Some of the bags swung heavily, no doubt with the dead bodies of babies. Ghosts and devils, monsters and ghouls, all of them ripped from the bowels of Hell to walk the Earth, feeding their lusts and desires.

She wanted to look away. She wanted to hide, but that would be weakness. She could not be weak. She pulled the curtain back a bit more so that she could see the entire block. The Harrisons had opened their door to a couple of small demons. The evil ones stood with their bags open, no doubt to collect the Harrison's souls. A small tear formed in the corner of Annie's eye. She did not want to see it any-more. The Harrisons were nice people. Sometimes they watched her while her parents left for an evening out. Why must they lose their souls? Why weren't they fighting like Momma and Daddy?

She wanted to look away, to turn a blind eye to the evils which befell her neighbors, but that would not do. A good Christian would not turn away in the face of evil. A good Christian would stand strong, would not waver in the face of such darkness. When at last the demons had collected the payment from the Harrisons, they turned and walked away, moving up the block to the next house.

The Steins seemed like nice enough people, but Annie was not surprised to see the devils coming to their house. After all, they were Jews. Momma had told her about Jews, Muslims, Buddhists and all of the other false religions. They were doomed to be tortured in the pits of Hell because they had not yet accepted Jesus into their hearts. Annie had tried from time to time to convince the Steins that they must believe in the power of Christ. Mr. and Mrs. Stein had three children. Didn't they have a responsibility to keep their son and daughters safe? They wouldn't listen though; they would just pat her on the head and send her home. It had become clear to Annie that they did not want to be saved for some reason; they had accepted their condemnation to the pit.

The demon rang their doorbell. The door opened to reveal Mr. Stein dressed head to toe in black and orange. He laughed at the little demon. From within a bowl, he produced something and dropped it into the monster's bag. He reached out and patted the vile thing on the head, just as he had patted Annie so many times before. A shudder ran through her body.

She opened the curtains a bit more so that she might see what else was happening on this demon filled night. Who else had fallen prey to the evil ways of the monsters which filled the street? The cul-de-sac was filled to the brim with them. The monsters had invaded every single stoop and doorstep. The only souls which were safe were those within her house. She scanned the faces of the creatures. So varied, some of them didn't even look like they were all that dangerous, but therein lay the danger. The Devil and his minions were not beyond tricks. They made themselves look so nice and kind. They made themselves look like nothing more than children at play.

Then she saw him. She knew it was him. Who else could it be? The horns, the hair. She thought he would be red as she had seen him drawn in so many pictures. He looked so human. It was shocking. He wore a golden crown on his head. The horns were long and pointed, or so she thought. They were at least so on the crown. Perhaps they were short and stubby beneath. His hair was long and black; it was slick and shiny. His body was wrapped in the robes of a king, green and black with flecks of gold. In his left hand, he held a bladed scepter. It was not the pitchfork she had imagined but it was not far off. No doubt the tales of him had been exaggerated. In his right hand, he held the biggest bag she had seen the whole night. It was weighted down by only God knew what. He was mesmerizing. His robes swirled about him as he made his way from door to door.

He must have known she was looking. He must have felt her eyes upon him. He turned to face her. From the street, he pointed with his scepter right at her. The demons, which surrounded him, turned to look. There was an enormous beast, green from head to toe, wearing purple shorts. Another had long blonde hair and carried in his hand a hammer, no doubt for the breaking in of doors and the smashing of heads. Then there was the one draped in the American flag. He was the worst of them, trying to hide behind the colors of the greatest nation in the world. Another was made of metal, red as a demon should be, and a woman in tight, black leather who surely used her feminine wiles to seduce men into the pit. Then there was the hunter, his quiver full of arrows. They turned and looked, following the line of his scepter. They had all seen her. There would be no more hiding.

They started her way. God, what was she to do. She let the curtains go and ran for her door. She flung it open and ran into the hallway, turning left for Momma and Daddy's room. Three steps were all it had taken for her to get to the door. She raised her hand to knock on the door when she heard the voice almost a whisper from beyond the hard wood.

"Christ, yes, fill me up!"

It was Momma. Their first bout against the demons must not have worked. They were still fighting. She could hear pounding against the wall. The demons must have breached the house. She knew if she knocked, there was a chance she might distract Momma and Daddy from their work. They might be lost to the powers of the demons.

She had to fight. She had to be like them. Back to her room she ran, knowing they would be upon her soon. Just as she shut her bedroom door behind her, the doorbell rang. It was more insistent this time, the ringing coming in quicker succession; then came the pounding. They must have all been at it. They seemed prepared to break the doors down. From outside, she could hear a cacophony of voices chanting their evil magic, "Trick or treat, trick or treat, trick or treat."

She lifted her *Bible* from her bed and held it to her chest. Annie began the chants she had heard from Momma and Daddy so many times before.

"Please, God! Fill me up. Christ, I need you inside me. Yes! Yes! God, Jesus. I can feel you, deep inside me. Deeper! Deeper! More, Jesus, more."

Her prayer was broken by the sound of feet landing on her balcony. Oh God, they were just outside the doors to her room. What was she going to do?

Then came the tapping, a mocking sound. They knew she was inside.

"Come on," said a deep voice from outside. "We know you are in there. Trick or Treat."

Again, the tapping on the window.

He wanted her. She knew it. A trophy to take back

down to the pit.

"Open the door," came the deep voice.

She had to face him. The *Bible* would protect her. She took small steps toward the doors. Throwing back the curtain, she stared the Devil in the eyes. He looked to be only a couple of years older than she, but it was another one of the Devil's tricks.

He smiled a crooked smile, all shining white teeth. "Hey, open up."

She reached for the door handle, holding the *Bible* tight in her right hand. With a sweaty palm, she pulled down on the handle, releasing the lock. As the door opened wide, she cocked back her right arm. Annie released the handle of the door and swung the *Bible* at the Devil with all of her might, chanting the words of Momma and Daddy under her breath. Her eyes were closed but she could tell that she had struck a hard blow with the spine of her *Bible*. Whatever she hit was soft and squishy. There was a crunch which echoed in her ears. She opened her eyes to find the Devil clutching at its throat. The scepter and bag had dropped to the ground. A strained attempt at breathing came from the throat of the beast.

Annie stepped forward and swung the *Bible* again, striking yet another blow for the almighty Christ. She knocked the crown from the Devil's head.

He backpedaled, attempting to escape the powerful hand of the Lord. The Devil hit the small wood railing with such momentum that he broke a piece free and tumbled to the ground below, landing on his head. He lay on the ground in a heap.

The other demons ran toward their master. The female screamed as she knelt beside the limp form of her leader.

The big green one yelled, "Tim!" over and over again.

The doors of the neighbors' houses flew open and they poured out into the street to see the work of God, to see the

Devil beaten and broken.

Annie's heart filled with pride. She couldn't wait for Momma and Daddy to see what she had done.

The Devil had come to tempt her and she had cast him out.

BY THE BOOK

By Kate Jonez

A draft swirls through the room which was once a parlor but is now a living room. A room for the living. The breeze lifts the filmy curtains which should be, to be true to Victorian motif, heavy and velvet. The white sheers are all that's left of Bridget's authentic Victorian window treatment. They float into the room like Ophelia's veils in the river.

The night is too cold for Halloween. Concerned mothers will force their kids to ruin their costumes by stuffing winter coats under their witch dresses or Superman tights. The few mothers who still let their kids trick-or-treat, that is. The cold air is thin. It is a sign that the time is right. The veil between this world and the next must also be thin.

Bridget's living room, which takes up nearly half the space in the first floor apartment of the old Victorian she rents, is as tidy as a photo in a *Pottery Barn* catalog. On this particular Halloween eve, it is even more tidy than usual. She has child-proofed it. Every carpet is taped down to prevent falls. No glass knick-knack or sharp-edged object is within reach of anyone under five foot ten. Plastic bags are hidden from every living thing and even the electrical outlets are protected against the insertion of the stray knife or fork.

A week ago Bridget had posted a flyer advertising her services as a mother's helper on the bulletin board in the very same library where she had found *the book*. Fewer parents than she had expected stopped by to interview her. Seems like parents would be more enthusiastic about such a fastidious babysitter. Especially one willing to work on a holiday. Perhaps they sensed she was trying too hard. So far, she'd only gotten one customer.

One is all she needs.

"That picture of you is creepy," Roderick says.

He bounces on her Chinoiserie-print settee with his arms wrapped around his knees and his shoes on the cushion. He's a chubby boy with red-hair and freckles. It's easy to see the balding, overweight, inconsiderate man he will become.

Bridget wants to kill him.

She's going to kill him tonight when the clock strikes midnight, but if she does it now the task will be over and his nasty little shoes won't be ruining her expensive furniture. She probably should wait until midnight, though. Everything by *the book.*

According to mysterious volume that had appeared on the shelf at the branch library between *Victorian Designs for the Home* by Newton, Charles and *Introduction to Victorian Style* by Crowley, David, midnight on All Hallows Eve is the only night of the year when the veil to the otherworld is thin enough to breach. Why would a book like this appear on her favorite shelf? Britney had obviously put it there? There is no other explanation. Her twin longs to return.

The language in the book had been a bit old-fashioned and dense. Bridget had to look up many of the words. Anything worth doing takes effort. She'd pored over the book for months until it became clear what she had to do.

"That is not me." Bridget glances at the studio portrait of Britney. Their appearance is identical. In every other possible way they are different. Britney is the friendly one, the trusting one, the sexy one—the dead one.

The ghostly sheer curtain catches a draft and wafts into

the room. The veil is thin, Britney. The veil is thin tonight. Bridget and Britney will be together again.

The photo's intricately carved frame is beautiful. The photo looks all wrong. It should be in sepia tones. She remembers her sister that way. She has to. The colors are too vivid otherwise. Remembering Britney's colors will make her come undone, and that can never happen again.

"It looks like you." Roderick's feet slide off the cushion and thump on the floor. He propels himself across the room and comes to an abrupt stop in front of Britney's portrait. "Except something is weird about her eyes."

Roderick's mother warned Bridget about the child's hyperactivity disorder. She had also said he was prone to putting non-food items in his mouth. Seems an odd thing for a seven-year-old to do, but at least he wouldn't suffer with his afflictions much longer.

Somehow, Bridget will have to deliver the news of Roderick's demise to his mother. That is a troubling thought. She is not sure what she will say. The best solution is to let Britney tell her. Britney is good with people.

"She looks like me because we are twins." Bridget says.

The words sounded redundant. She had never before had to explain her status. Everyone, or at least everyone who matters, knows she's a twin. She's the polite one. The cautious one. The serious one. No wonder Bridget feels off-kilter. Together she and Britney are two halves of a balanced whole. Alone nothing is as it should be.

"Her eyes look otherworldly because she is dead." Bridget says. The picture is called a memento mori. With the advent of photography, Victorians took up the habit of photographing deceased family members to create keepsakes. The practice has fallen out of favor in—"

"For real dead?" Roderick's eyes display the first spark of curiosity Bridget has seen.

"Yes."

"How come she died?" Roderick touches the bowed glass of the portrait. Bridget thinks about telling him to keep his fingers to himself, but she holds her tongue. She'll give her apartment a thorough cleaning tomorrow.

His question is rude and inappropriate. In spite of its thoughtlessness, Bridget prefers it to the fake sympathy and forced condolences most people offer. The answer to that question ultimately lies in Britney's nature. She was the friendly one, the trusting one, the sexy one. That is an open invitation for disaster. How come, indeed?

A glimmer of white behind the leg of the settee catches Bridget's eye. The tiny globe rolls and rolls until it runs out of momentum and stops. Another... It's definitely a sign.

"You will be afraid if I tell you. It is not an appropriate story for children."

"You can tell me. I played Grand Theft Auto once." Roderick plops down on the edge of her Queen Anne chair. He bounces up and down.

"This is real, not a game."

"I know that." He fiddles with a tassel on a pillow, almost stands up again, and then falls back. It is probably a symptom of that condition his mother described, but it looks more like some sort of existential angst. Roderick craves something true, some sliver of truth unfiltered.

Roderick reaches over the leather bound book Bridget found at the library, *the book*, and past the kitchen knife, a stand-in for an athame, and reaches for the plate on the table without asking. "Do these have nuts? I'm allergic to nuts." He grabs one of the soul cakes, which are actually tiny pies in spite of their name, and without even acknowledging the beauty of the star shaped lattice work of the crust he shoves it in his mouth.

Bridget lowers herself onto the settee. She tries to assume a casual air as she reaches down, but her movements are jerky and halting. For some reason she doesn't want this child to know what she is doing. She doesn't want to let him know how thin the veil is or how hopeless his situation.

"Ewww," Roderick cups his hand under his mouth and spits. "Nuts, nuts, nuts!" He hops to his feet and jumps up and down as though he has to urinate. He holds the handful of chewed up mush at arm's length.

While Roderick is occupied with jumping, Bridget snatches up the pearl and slips it into the pocket of her cardigan.

Sixteen. This one makes sixteen.

Bridget rushes to the powder room and retrieves the waste receptacle and a damp towel.

"Discard that." She holds out the basket and waits for Roderick to comply. She wipes his hand.

"I'm going to die. My air passages are constricting." Roderick gasps and clutches his throat. He staggers against the wall like a victim in a horror movie. The movement is a reasonably good re-enactment of how her sister fell. Britney too clutched her throat and made gurgling and wheezing noises. In Britney's case the sounds weren't caused by constricted air passages. Britney's air passages were severed. Separated. Cut clean through. The forensic examiner, thinking no family members were close by had speculated about what might be holding her head on her body.

Roderick will not get to perform the scene to full dramatic effect. For that he would need to tangle himself in the velvet curtains Bridget discarded when the cleaners couldn't get the blood from Britney's arterial spray out of the gold velvet.

"No one ever expired from eating nuts."

Bridget tilts her head. She hears it. The rolling sound. She hears it again even over Roderick's commotion.

Roderick stops stumbling and clutching his throat as though his theatrics were a sweater he could put on or take off as needed. "Yes they do too," he says. "My mom got the principal to ban them from my school."

The sound persists. It doesn't grow louder or softer. It persists.

"I suppose that makes you especially popular with the other children."

Roderick stops mid-gasp. He narrows his eyes and studies Bridget. "They are just a bunch of bullies anyway."

"If you weren't such a monstrous little yob, maybe the kids would like you better."

The boy's mouth falls open and his eyes grow large. "I'm telling my mom what you said. No one likes a potty mouth."

Bridget doesn't bother to respond. He won't be telling his mother anything. Not on this night, or ever again.

Bridget has never been able to locate the source of the pearls. They come from the general direction of the window with the missing curtain.

Finally it rolls into view. With the deliberation and unswerving inevitability of a train on a track, it comes to rest against the toe of her shoe. This one has a drip of lurid red.

Seventeen.

How many pearls make a necklace?

Roderick no longer gasps or clutches at his throat. His nut allergy seems to have not been that serious after all. He clutches his fists. His face is a little on the pink side, but he does not in fact appear to be dying. "Do you have any candy? Kids are supposed to get candy on Halloween."

"I made the soul cakes."

"Those are gross."

"Children aren't just handed candy on Halloween. They must to go out and trick-or-treat for it."

"That's too dangerous. The world isn't safe for kids these days."

"Is that your opinion?"

"My mom says that. She said you were going to do fun stuff for Halloween. I sure would like to know when that's going to start."

"You've never been trick or treating?"

Roderick sighs like a world-weary old man. "No. I think it'd be worth the risk, but my mom says no."

"She's probably right. We'll have to respect her wishes."

Roderick's face twitches like his insides are clockwork and someone has wound the key. "How come your sister died?" he asks once his face has tried on several expressions.

"Someone murdered her."

Roderick's mouth falls open and his eyes grow large and round as is his custom, it seems, when faced with reality. "Where?"

"Right here in this very room. In front of the window." Bridget lets her eyes float along with the curtain. "A man who was visiting her got mad and slashed her throat then stabbed her over and over until he stuck his knife in her heart."

Roderick's breathing is a little irregular. His face looks a bit sweaty and pale.

"Was there blood everywhere?"

"Yes."

"Did you see it all happen?"

"Yes I did."

The sound is different this time. A pearl bounces before it rolls. Without moving her head, Bridget scans the floor.

"What did you do?" Roderick stops fidgeting. He stares at her, his childish cheeks flushed pink.

"What do you mean, what did I do? I was a witness."

Another pearl bounces then rolls. Still she can't see it.

"You didn't try to stab him or shoot him or jump on his back or anything?"

Bridget opened her mouth to respond. Why had this

idea never occurred to her before?

Pearls fall in slow motion, one after another. They bounce and roll just like they did on that night.

Bridget jumps up. The light grows hazy and bright. Her head tingles. She should have fought him. She should have done something. Is that it Britney?

Pearls cascade and roll in every direction.

"Candy!" Roderick dives to the floor. He grabs a handful of pearls and shoves them in his mouth.

"No!" Bridget lunges for him. She grabs him around the waist, heaves him up and shoves her fingers in his mouth. "Spit them out." Her voice is high-pitched and panicky. It's not at all like the soothing tone she'd practiced for her babysitting interviews. She shakes him until he spits out the pearls.

"Bad touch! Bad touch. Stranger danger!" Roderick squeals.

"Quiet." Bridget places him on the floor. "I didn't hurt you."

He scuttles backward like a cornered cat until he hits the wall. "I want my mommmmm. I want to go home."

That is not at all the plan for this Halloween eve. Bridget glances down at her athame, her candles placed just so and *the book,* the miraculous book that tells her everything she must do to bring Britney back.

Roderick cuts his wail short when the doorbell rings.

"Don't move." Bridget points her finger at Roderick just like the wicked witch she's become.

The moment she pulls the door open, Roderick lets loose a whoop and charges for freedom. He streams through the door and out into the night knocking down the small visitor standing on the porch.

"Are you okay?" Bridget holds out her hand to help the child up.

"Trick-or treat," he says through the slit in his plastic

mask and holds open a pillowcase.

Bridget scans the street. Roderick has rounded a corner and is nowhere to be seen. No one else is on the street waiting or watching.

"Come inside. Would you like to try a soul cake?"

The little boy steps over the threshold and Bridget closes the door behind him."

Any child will do.

ANKOU, KING OF THE DEAD

By R.B. Payne

Brittany, France.
1562 A.D.

Dusk envelopes the village of Morlaix as the first frigid sea-wind of winter slices through the lingering warmth of autumn. From the black soil of harvested fields, a fog rises and drifts to the cemetery at the village center.

You step inside your stone hut and close the oaken door.

It is Octobre 31st.

All Hallows Evening.

A dangerous night.

At midnight the souls of the dead rise from their cold graves and return to the warmth of their former homes.

You must prepare.

From the cloth-covered larder you take a flagon of ale and a meat pie. You lay them on an embroidered cloth next to sweetened breads and a roasted apple.

Later, you will leave your door open to receive the spirits. You won't be able to see them but you'll know they've arrived by a crackle of the flame in the hearth, the creak of the thatched roof, or a wispy movement of a curtain.

The spirits will feast until Ankou, the King of the Dead, comes to collect their souls and escort them to the Otherworld.

But if you, one of the living, are accidentally caught by

Ankou, his scythe may touch you and you will be harvested with the dead.

Gone from this world.

A shiver passes through you.

No one has ever seen Ankou and lived to tell the tale. He is reputed to be a tall skeleton whose skull constantly turns in a circle seeking the souls of the dead.

He wears a peasant's hat and cape, and carries a scythe.

Sometimes he wears a death shroud.

He comes to collect the souls of those who have died in the previous year but he will take the souls of the living if he catches them unawares.

In the darkness of All Hallows Evening, Ankou stands atop a creaky wagon pulled by two horses and passes through the villages of Brittany. He sweeps his scythe forward, the dull edge collecting all souls that cross his path. The captured souls are piled in his wagon, one spiritual corpse upon another.

In preparation for their journey to the Otherworld, the souls of your family will first return to your hut.

Your wife. Your daughter. Your son.

They died when the rats came last spring.

You will make your family welcome while they wait for Ankou.

There is a banging at your door.

"Who is it?" you whisper.

"Bastian," says a hushed voice.

Time for Black Vespers.

~

"We live with our dead," the priest says in Latin. "On this All Hallows Evening let the blessedness of death be praised. Let us ponder the meaning of sorrows and the shortness of life. Let us pray and give thanks for the harvest."

The parishioners bow their heads.

You make the Sign of the Cross. Although you are now Catholic, you remember the tales of ancient times told by your father.

Long ago this land was called Armorica but all that is left of those people are the stacked stones called *menhirs* and *dolmen*. They often weigh more than a hundred horses, their sacred purpose lost in the passing of time.

Later, this land was Celtic. It was a time when people worshiped the wind, sun, and moon. The Gods and Goddesses had powers of air, fire, and water. In those days the people celebrated Samhain: the festival of summer's end.

Then the Romans came with Roman gods. Pluto, God of the Underworld, and his ferryman: Charon.

When the Romans left, the land of Armorica was given by Emperor Maximus to Cynan Meridoc, a warrior-king from the land of Britain. He named the land Brittany.

Little Britain.

The land of your birth.

As the Holy Mass ends, you walk with Bastian through the darkened village. Nearby, in the graveyard, a stone tower stands high above the headstones. On its roof, the *lanterns des morts* sparkle, trying to keep the night-wandering spirits near their graves until the proper time.

As you pass the cemetery entrance your hand brushes a row of stacked skulls. These were other villagers, dug up over the years to make room for the newly dead. Next to the skulls is a crypt full of human bones.

A procession appears, led by the priest. Villagers are carrying buckets of fresh milk into the cemetery.

Using a ladle you pour milk onto the grave where your family is buried.

The milk will arouse them.

Wake up.

Time to feast.

It is All Hallows Evening.

~

You walk homeward, tired, aching, weak.

Footsteps approach.

Afraid, you turn to run, but from the darkness appears Tanguy, a traveling minstrel from Gaul. He has come to entertain the villagers and earn a free meal.

You follow him and enjoy the song that he plays on the *harpe de gourde* to call the villagers.

"Listen," Tanguy says when the villagers have gathered. "In honor of All Hallows Evening, I will tell the Tale of Ankou, and how he came to be the King of Death."

A cold wind makes you cough until your chest aches. You spit something dark to the ground and lean against a stone wall for support.

In flickering torchlight, Tanguy prances among the villagers as he recounts the story.

"Once, there was cruel Prince who loved to gamble and hunt. In a forest on his lands, there lived a magical White Stag and one evening the Prince decided to hunt the stag for it was told that killing the animal would mark the beginning of an extraordinary adventure. He mounted his favorite horse, and armed with bow and arrow, went to hunt. The Prince loved killing, and the moment of death, whether animal or man, was like mother's milk to him.

"He searched high and low for the stag. Bursting through the brush, the Prince halted, for blocking his way, was a massive figure cloaked in black on a magnificent white stallion.

"'Who goes there?' challenged the Prince. The hooded stranger did not answer and would not give way.

"The Prince would not retreat, for it was his land, and so he challenged the stranger to a contest. Whoever could kill the stag would not only keep the meat and the hide but he could also determine the fate of the loser.

"'Agreed,' said the stranger, his voice like autumn leaves

scraping against a castle wall.

"The hunt was over so quickly that the Prince could only stammer [sic]. As hard as he had ridden, the stranger had galloped faster. Through field, and stream, and mountain, the dark stranger remained in the lead, the cold night winds tugging wildly at his cloak. At last they saw the White Stag, but while the Prince was still stringing his bow, the stranger let his arrow loose with a whistle and a sickening tear of shredding flesh.

"The White Stag was dead. Angry, the Prince aimed an arrow at the heart of the hooded stranger.

"The stranger laughed, unafraid, 'I have won. You can have the stag and all the dead of the world. Your joy is hunting? Hunt then. Your trophies will be found across battlefields and hearth, and they will reek of decay, huntsman. From now on you must hunt the dead.' Before the Prince could speak, the stranger disappeared. And that's how the Prince became Ankou, King of the Dead. Now run home before he finds you."

Tanguy wails and sends the villagers scurrying.

You hurry home.

~

Death, are you kind or cruel?

You hide, curled, beneath a blanket on a filthy bed of hay. The door of your hut is open to the blackness of night.

You await the spirits.

The fire in your hearth has nearly gone out but you are afraid to stoke it.

A cold wind rustles the straw on the floor.

You peek. The cloth on the larder flutters revealing a solitary cup of porcelain.

Your wife is here.

It was her only treasure and she has come to see it one last time.

From somewhere you hear the laughter of children.

They must be playing outside.

You weep. You will be so alone when their souls have gone to the Otherworld.

From down the road comes the clanking of a wagon and the plodding of horses.

Ankou is coming.

The sound of the horses draws nearer and you gather the meager blanket closer. The clanking stops and you hear the snort of horses and the stamp of hooves on the ground.

Ankou must not see you.

Howling wind whips into your hut blowing loose straw into the hearth. The straw roars into flame so high you are afraid it will set your thatched roof on fire.

A blast of wind down the chimney extinguishes the fire plunging your hut into darkness.

The clanking of the wagon disappears down the road; your family is on their way to the Otherworld.

You fall into a fitful sleep and wake to the light of early morning.

All Hallows Evening is over.

Feeling a mixture of happiness and sadness, you walk to the cemetery to visit your family's grave.

You can't read the Latin inscription above the cemetery entrance but you know it says "Remember thou must die."

Your life is nearing its end.

You are twenty-seven years old.

You cough and spit yellow phlegm to the dirt. Breathing is hard and you have no appetite.

You realize that on the next All Hallows Evening, Ankou will be coming for you.

Further Reading

Evans-Wentz, W. Y. *The Fairy-Faith in Celtic Countries.* Minneapolis: Dover Publications, Incorporated, 2003. 218-21.

Kelley, Ruth Edna. *The Book of Hallowe'en.* Morrisville, NC: Lulu.com, 2007. 77-83.

Koch, John T. *Celtic Culture : A Historical Encyclopedia.* Danbury: ABC-CLIO, Incorporated, 2005. 67.

Le Braz, Anatole. *La légende de la mort chez les Bretons armoricains (The Legends of Death in Brittany).* Paris: H. Champion, 1902.

Morton, Lisa. *A Hallowe'en Anthology : Literary and Historical Writings over the Centuries.* Boston: McFarland & Company, Incorporated, 2008. 196,198.

MacCulloch, J. A. *The Religion of the Ancient Celts.* Edinburgh: T. & T. CLARK, 1911. 345.

Images

Ankou

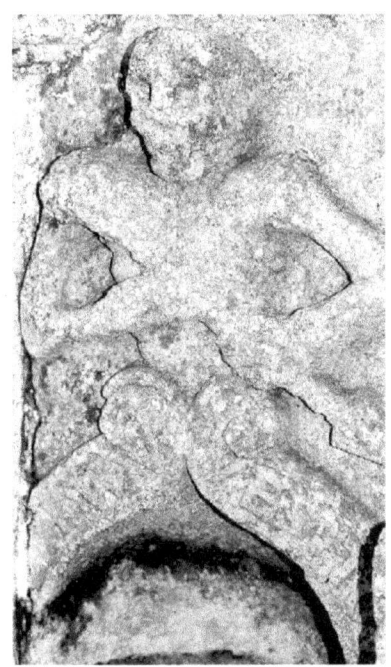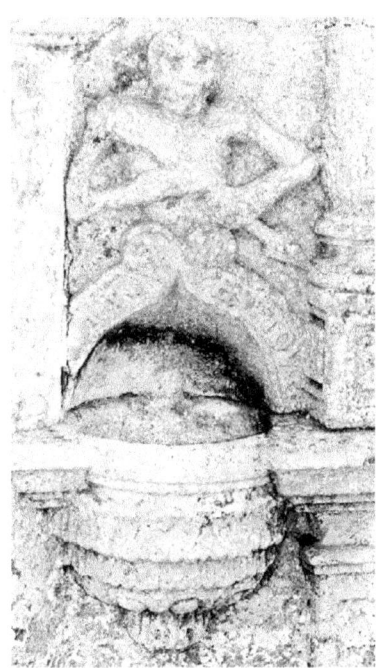

Sculpted carving of Ankou at the town of La Roche-
Maurice.

Skeleton, part of the sculpted funerary monument of
Philippa of Guelders, 1547

Ankou carved on a church.

Death as a skeleton carrying a scythe.

Le Petit Journal

LE CHOLÉRA

Death as Cholera.

THE LURKER

Steven W. Booth

For Querus

It's watching me again. The black cat. It stares through the window, motionless, all golden eyes and wind-ruffled fur. With its ragged right ear and jagged scar across the nose, I cannot help but see the face of malice.

It watches me every night for almost a month. I dream of it when I sleep. I feel my sanity is wearing away like autumn leaves blowing in the wind.

My wife chides me. "It's just an old black cat." She waves my mention of it away, as if it were simply a squeaky floorboard or a leaky faucet. "Probably belongs to one of the neighbors." When I don't respond, she chuckles. "It's not like you to be afraid of things in the dark."

The moment she mentions *fear*, I finally place a name on the tightening of my stomach, and the palpitations of my heart I experience whenever I see that cat. I am a grown man, after all, and I am *not* afraid of the dark, nor its inhabitants. But whenever that "old black cat" is near, looking in the window, watching me, I sense I truly have something to fear.

My wife, Melissa, and my two sons go to visit her parents for the weekend. It is Halloween tomorrow, and her folks live in a gated community with lots of other children.

It is safer than here, my wife and I agree. I would go, too, but I have to work on a project for a client this weekend, and I can't do that on the road. It is a sacrifice to be without them, one I am reluctant to make.

They kiss me goodbye and tell me how much they will miss me, and I of course will count the long hours until their return. Because when they are gone, there is nothing left here at home but me, that cat, and a sense of foreboding that I cannot shake.

Saturday morning and afternoon pass without incident. I do my work faster than usual without my family there to distract me. As the sun stretches down to the far mountains on the horizon, I settle in for the evening, and realize how lonely it is in this big house without others to fill it. It is nothing, I tell myself. I am a strong man, healthy and secure in my ability to defend myself from any physical attack. But the threat I sense is not physical. I feel as if my very soul is threatened.

The sky darkens, and the panic sets in. I call my in-law's house to tell my family I love them, but they are out trick-or-treating. I want them to know that they are my everything, and they need to know it now. There may not be an opportunity to express my feelings for them later.

A steaming mug of ginger tea calms my queasy stomach, the rich, bitter smell filling the room, but the hot liquid doesn't ease my tormented mind. I sit in my easy chair before the fire and breathe deeply, but my mind is still filled with images of the cat. I glance to the left, through the gap in the faded yellow curtains, and that cat is there, curse it! I stand and draw the curtains closed. It speaks, and I hear its mewling sounds of distress. For an instant, I feel sorry for it. The night is bitterly cold, and there it sits, on my sill, watching me. The cry is soft again, and I return to the window. *Should I help it?* I part the curtains and look out.

The black cat sees me and arches its back, expanding its fur in such a threatening pose that I recoil. The hiss is loud through the glass. It jumps at me, slamming into the window pane, and I stumble into a wall tripping over the footrest that stands before the fire.

"Son of a bitch!"

I hear scraping outside, and a growl less feline than demonic. I peer out through the curtains again, but the cat isn't there. It is below the window, trying to get in, trying to get to me.

I step away from the window again, and go to the fireplace. Ordinarily the glow would cheer me, but I feel nothing but ice in my bowels. Beside it is a poker, wholly unnecessary for our gas fireplace, but decorative and until now, useless. I pick it up. It is heavy and pointed, with a long, wicked hook near the end. I can't believe that I'm preparing to do battle with a cat, but I can hear it digging under the house, clanging into things in the basement.

I run to the kitchen, poker at the ready. I wonder if a carving knife might not be a better defense—or perhaps an open can of tuna—but almost immediately I hear the cat scratching at the basement door.

"Go away!" I back up into the butcher's block, which halts my retreat. "Leave me alone!"

The scratching is louder at the threshold, then abruptly stops. *Is it gone?*

But I know it has not gone. Instead it is looking for another way inside. I hear a noise in the air ducts. It is coming for me.

The panic, which I momentarily mastered, returns like an arctic wind. The cat is nearby, its presence almost palpable. I back away from the basement door, and listen to the sounds in the house. For a moment, the silence is enormous and seems to crush me. Then a scrabbling sound to my right makes me jump. It is in the air duct in the hallway to the bedrooms. That's where it will enter. And that's where I must face it.

My hands tremble, and I grip the poker until my knuckles are white. Am I really afraid of a cat? But I sense this is no simple beast. I have nothing but an iron poker to fend off the evil that haunts me.

The hallway is pitch black. I reach for the light switch, but when I turn it on, there is a loud *pop!* and an infinitely bright flash of light. In that one instant, I can see myself reflected in the framed art print at the end of the hall. Just behind me in the reflection is the face of a demon with yellow eyes and long fangs. I cry out and turn to see it for myself, but the darkness is upon me again. The scratching at the air duct grating becomes louder, and I know that the cat is almost inside.

I retreat to the living room. The table lamp is still on in there, and the fire is still going. I clutch the poker with both hands. The pain in my knuckles from gripping the weapon keeps me in my own skin. I don't know why this foe, this cat, has put such fear in my soul.

"What did I do to you?" I call out into the darkened hallway. The scrabbling sound at the grating has ceased, and I hear a low, rumbling growl, unmistakably feline. The black cat emerges from the darkness, golden eyes glowing in the firelight.

"Stay away," I shout, and I swing the poker menacingly.

The cat stalks closer, each paw silent, its eyes focus on me, boring through me.

"Leave me alone!" I scream. Terror clasps its icy hands around my heart, and I feel faint with it. But I must stand my ground. I must!

"What do you want from me?" I whisper as it approaches even nearer. "Please," I beg. "Please go away!"

The cat—if that's what it truly is—lowers its head, tail swishing. Before I can say anything else, it leaps at me, and

I scream. Its claws dig into my shoulder, tearing the flesh beneath my shirt. The searing pain of its touch shocks me with its intensity. Next, I know, the demon beast will be at my throat.

But the cat doesn't tear out my windpipe, as I fear. Instead, it bounds over my shoulder, and yowls, crashing into something behind me.

I spin and there, standing as close to me as my own shadow, is a low, crouching creature, twisted and evil, with greenish-black flesh the color of death, and a red, contorted mouth as bright as lava. The long talons on its hands are upon the cat as they fight. This thing, this horror, can only be the Devil himself. And that cat has attached itself to Satan's face, teeth and claws sinking deeply into the sickly flesh. From Satan's throat comes a shout of anguish beyond my darkest imaginings, and I know true fear for the first, and probably the last, time.

But the cat won't let go, no matter how deeply the Devil's talons sink into it. The cat shrieks and digs deeper into Satan's face. The demon tries to shake off his tormentor, but he cannot. He turns and stumbles over the footrest and tumbles into the fire. The cat, bleeding and singed, howls in pain, yet it still won't retreat. The demon's dark fur is set ablaze for a moment, the fire dancing on its skin, but is quickly extinguished. I can hear the cat's life being squeezed out of it by Satan's crushing claws. The cat takes a deep breath, but instead of resuming the attack, it gives the most piteous meow I could ever wish to hear. The cat, I know, is dying in the act of protecting me. And it is about to lose.

Something about the sound of the cat's cry brings me back to myself. I am a man, I am armed, and I am *letting a cat fight for me?* I know deep in my being that if I let the cat die in the act of saving me, and yet I survive, I will have lost my soul as surely as if the Devil himself had taken it from me.

The time to hesitate has come and gone. It is now the moment for me to act, perhaps my last.

I raise the poker over my head, poised to strike. Satan shakes his head like a rabid dog, and the cat flies from its grip. I bring the poker down, driving the hook squarely between Satan's brows. Instead of crying out, the Devil looks at me and meets my eyes for the first time. His gaze is one of hate, of evil, and for the briefest of instants, I wonder why he is here and what he wants with me. But I am done doubting myself. I raise the poker again, and hit him once more, this time in the throat. Black blood, absent in the wound in his head, gushes forward and burns my flesh. I shrink away, but my gaze falls on the cat, laying there, exhausted and wounded.

I raise the poker once more, this time hitting the demon in the heart. The blood that spouts like a fountain from his throat ceases spraying, and Satan's eyes, until then brimming with malice, become blank and dead.

I stand there for a moment, wondering if it is a ruse. I have no idea how to tell if Satan is really dead. But then I hear the cat's labored breathing, and I know that I must attend to my savior, even at the risk of my own life.

I drop the poker, the handle clanking loudly on the hardwood floor, and run to the cat that lies in the corner, its side barely rising and falling. I kneel beside it, this cat that has saved me. I put my hands on it, and it flinches, but then relaxes. It seems to understand that I am there to help it, as it has helped me.

Its eyes turn to me, barely open, and it purrs under my touch. I stroke it softly, and praise it wordlessly. I need to get it some help, get it to the hospital. And I need to leave this cursed place as soon as I can.

I lift it gently, and cradle the small form in my arms. Its eyes close halfway, and I think it will sleep. Instead, it looks beyond me, and hisses.

I hold the cat protectively to my breast and spin to see Satan on his feet, chuckling at me, at my conceit that I thought I could kill him.

But I am done fearing him. I have the cat to protect, and my life is nothing compared to that.

"You're not welcome here," I try to sound stern, but I'm not sure I am successful.

"I'm not welcome anywhere. Why should this place be different?"

"What do you want?"

"You," he grins, his jagged, broken teeth yellow and black with decay.

"You can't have me."

"Oh, I don't know. Every man has his price." Satan's sickly-sweet grin is unnerving. "I have it! If you come with me, I will save the cat's life."

I shudder. "And if I say no?"

"Both of you will come."

I hesitate for the barest of instants. I owe the cat my life and more. It is a high price, but is it too high?

The hesitation takes too long. The cat bites me on the hand. I glare down at it, and it growls at me.

I look up. "You cannot take what is not yours," I say with as much conviction as I can muster.

"Then you are mine." He takes a broad, three-toed step forward.

"Not today. You can kill me, but you cannot have me." I place my hand over the cat's body as it rests in my other arm. "I..." Then the words come to my mind. "I banish you." It is a stall, nothing more, but what else have I in my arsenal against the Devil?

Satan looks surprised. "You banish me?" And he bellows with sarcastic mirth, a baritone, resonant sound filled with so much evil I shudder. He cocks his head to the side. "What does that even mean?"

I don't have an answer, but the fear in my heart has left me.

"There's nothing for you here, now, Satan." I take a step forward. "The only thing you have taken from me is my fear of you. I should thank you, I think."

Now it is the Devil's turn to hesitate. "Thank me?" He seems to fade a bit. "Thank *me*?"

The cat's teeth pinch my finger, but I don't need a stronger hint this time.

"Thank you," I say, and he grows a bit dimmer. "Thank you for showing me what is truly important."

Satan's face twists, and his jagged teeth press into a horrific scowl. Large boils on his cheeks pulsate as if I am in imminent danger from the eruption of villainous pus. He roars and fire flares from his mouth. Burning embers fall on my floor, singing my wife's new oriental, and the stench of charred carpet fills my nostrils. Instead of making me fear, I laugh.

"Thank you," I repeat. He was not much more than a wisp. He reaches out for me, and I smile. Who would guess that gratitude was the Devil's Achilles' heel? "Thank you," I murmur softly, and in my heart I mean that one for the cat.

A moment later, the Devil is no more. I take no chances, however. We have incense in my wife's bathroom. I light a bundle and spread the smoke everywhere, twice over. I don't care if incense and the Lord's Prayer are supposed to go together or not. The house is fragrant with the scent of sage, and we pray, something I hadn't done in so long I wonder if it will do anything at all. But I hadn't believed in the Devil before tonight, either.

When my wife and sons return the next evening, I have repaired the damage the fight had done to the house. The cat sits next to me, a bandage wrapped around its abdomen. He purrs as I stroke him.

"Who's this?" My wife asks as I stand and greet her, burrowing my head into her shoulders and soaking up that woodsy perfume in her hair. She smells like fresh apples, cinnamon, and a splash of zesty orange. "Your tormentor, I see."

"Yes, my tormentor," I rub my hand over his ragged ear.

"What happened to him?"

I look down at his bandage. "He got into a fight with a wild animal. But he should be fine soon."

"What's his name?" asks my oldest son, Robert.

I look at the cat for just a moment. I hadn't gone as far as to name him.

"How does Lucifer sound?"

My wife looks at me strangely, tilting her head and furrowing her brow. "Really? Isn't that a bit dark?"

"Not really." My smile starts slowly but I feel it filling my face. "He has brought me light, and I think the name fits."

Alex, my youngest son, approaches Lucifer, and strokes him gently on the head. Lucifer purrs and presses against Alex's hand.

"We should really love him, Dad. After all, Lucifer *is* the first angel of God."

I look at the boy, surprised. I didn't know that, or if I did, I had forgotten.

My wife smiles, but her look is still uncertain, hesitant even. "He's staying, I guess."

"Yes," I gaze into the molten gold of his eyes. "He is."

HARVEST OF FLAMES

By Maria Alexander

Name: Lupa

Breed: 80% Husky, 20% Wolf

Weight: 56 lbs.

Height: 30" at the shoulder

Chipped and Collared

(Inserted here is a photo of a wolf hybrid, with sandy fur and golden eyes that glow like simmering pools of metallic liquid. She gazes at the camera, her eyes stealing the soul of the photographer.)

Last seen: Runyon Canyon Park, Inspiration Point
10/26/14

A series of tabs etched with my name ("Nadya") and phone number fringe the notice, ready to be torn off by helpful Hollywood residents.

I lean against the telephone pole, sobbing as traffic purrs past. I have tried everything. Phoned every veterinarian's office and shelter within ten miles of my Hollywood apartment. SPCA. Animal Control. Walked for miles, leash in hand, calling her name. I've put up these notices everywhere I can in a three-mile radius. No luck. I no longer wonder if she's hurt. Instead, I worry someone has stolen her, mesmerized by those eyes. But is that possible? Because she's part wolf, she's not like other dogs. She doesn't bounce with joy, seeking approval from every stranger she meets. She hangs back and watches until she's sure that person is an ally. Her friendship is earned. Her loyalty a gift.

The morning I lost her, I had slipped out the front gate of my apartment building into an early October winter. Clouds of cold escaped our mouths. Lupa trotted beside me. Her soft pink tongue lolled in the brisk air, blackened lips grinning. As Lupa thrived, I shivered and cursed climate change.

We crossed Hollywood Boulevard—or Halloween Boulevard, as I like to call it because of the weirdoes—and hiked to the dog park in Runyon Canyon. Lupa loped several feet ahead on her leash.

The gate to the dog park provided a dusky entrance to the dirt paths that climbed uphill past trees with branches that groped the ground. I wouldn't have felt safe here without Lupa, despite all the preening Hollywood yuppies. Shady characters are always lurking on the paths beneath the trees. Los Angeles the ugly and terrible, author of hunger and havoc.

Lupa's nose danced in the direction of a gray terrier and then to a pair of bronze Weimaraners, yet further to a slender Dalmatian lapping noisily at a water faucet sputtering into a muddy patch. Although dogs at every turn yapped and snarled at one another, none so much as sniffed Lupa. I don't even call her Lupa in public for fear that someone will literally cry wolf and try to get her picked up by Animal Control. Gripping Lupa's leash tighter, I took a sharp turn up an especially steep path.

To Inspiration Point.

The towers of downtown Los Angeles turned a dark face toward the scattered lights of West Hollywood. The point ended at an open cliff. Dizzy yet excited by the heights, I inhaled the frigid air as Lupa sniffed circles around the outcropping. The hazy blue sky wrapped its spacious arms around us and the sun knelt behind the bristling ridge to our right. In twilight, Lupa did her business and I cleaned it up. We'd have to leave soon. The park was closing.

Otherworldly bells chimed in the copse of trees ahead of us.

Goosebumps raised on the flesh of my arms beneath my nylon jacket. I froze with terror, although I wasn't certain why. Lupa sat at attention, ears forward. She barked, throaty and loud. A squall abruptly slapped the trees. Strands of my long, black hair whipped into my face. The copse of trees fanned in the roaring wind. Shadows swarmed the rustling leaves.

Darkness flashed across the dirt outcropping. Lupa barked viciously. Her fur ruffled in the wind like fields of wheat. Then, she charged into the copse, leash ripping from my hands. I fell forward hard. Rocks and dead tree debris tore into my arms and knees. The dust from Lupa's running feet choked me.

"Lupa!"

Deaf to me, she scampered into the shadows, tail flicking between coiling boughs.

Don't chase the dog, I told myself. *She'll only run harder.* I, slowly, if not calmly, stepped into the shadows. Heart racing. Body stinging from the fall. I pulled my cell phone out of my pocket to use it as a flashlight as I called to Lupa. I heard nothing but the wind rattling the tree limbs, tearing away the remaining leaves. Los Angeles is evergreen, but this copse of trees seemed to die before my eyes.

I searched for hours. No Lupa.

Just darkness.

~

Tomorrow is Halloween.

Back at work, I sink into depression at my desk as I read artist contracts. I haven't slept much since Lupa disappeared. Friends flood my inbox with offers to help search, put up posters, call shelters. My colleagues are very sweet, lending encouragement. I even found a card from my boss this morning. He lost his cat Gracie once. He understands.

A knock on my office door.

"Come in."

It's Marjan. Short and trim. Long wavy dark hair and deep brown eyes. She leans in the doorway. "Are you okay?"

I nod. Face heating. Heart breaking. "I'll be okay. It's hard to concentrate sometimes."

"I bet." Marjan rubbed her arms vigorously. "What is up with the cold? Did you bring back some weather from Ireland?"

The memory warmed me. "You know what I wish I'd brought back."

"Cradle robber," Marjan teased, winking. "Hey, you want to get some lunch?"

~

Icy wind blasted our tour group as we climbed stone steps to the majestic Cliffs of Moher. Below, the Atlantic Ocean swirled against the shore, lapis and pearl. The other tourists on the bus had made fun of me for my earmuffs and hat this last week of April, but now they praised my wise packing. One of the tourists was a young, handsome philosophy graduate. He offered to take my picture.

"What a lovely camera," Jack said with that charming Welsh accent. He turned over the equipment admiringly in a gloved hand. His green eyes flickered, shyly glimpsing at me through shaggy red bangs. Even the second day of *the bus tour, he could scarcely look me in the eye—ironic because I could hardly stop looking at him. He couldn't have been more than twenty-two. I was ten years older.*

"It was a gift," I said. My boyfriend Damon gave it to me last Christmas. Damon, who never wanted to go to Ireland and backed out of even taking me to the airport at the last minute. Damon, who had offered to take Lupa but informed me that he couldn't two days before my trip. Damon, with whom I needed to break up.

For a while, I thought Damon and I would get married and have children. My parents are always pushing me about that. Yet it never works out. I tell them, maybe I'm not meant to get married and have kids. Maybe that's not my destiny.

Jack's smooth pink lips curled up on one side of his mouth. He lifted the camera to his eye.

I posed under the arch of a small castle outpost, an ancient rook crowned with battlements over four hundred years old, moss tingeing the rugged dun stone. I placed my bare hands on the cool, rough surface. Knowing he was looking at me, I smiled.

~

I think of young Jack often.

Marjan and I work at an art gallery in Westwood Village. Our clientele is mostly young Persian couples. Just a block away is Persian Square, the area bordering Westwood Boulevard that's filled with shops dedicated to our Iranian clients. Those same clients find their way to our gallery and purchase the pastoral scenes that our artists produce. I've helped Marjan put together some successful exhibits. Pretty exciting considering so many shops are closing in this area.

We walk side-by-side on Broxton, heading to our favorite Mongolian barbecue. UCLA students swarm the boba teahouses and burger joints, pecking at their phones as they stumble blindly down the sidewalk. Yawning, Marjan talks about her small kids, complaining that she can't get them to bed at night. She relates far too much to that picture book for adults, *Go the F@ck to Sleep.*

I'm distracted by the Halloween decorations. The Village certainly gets its "ghost" on this time of year with cottony spider webbing strung up across the merchandise displays. Even the "Aaahs!" store, normally devoted to TV and sports fandom, clutters its windows with tacky Halloween costumes, sticking witch hats on the manikins. Students crowd in front of the gaudy Halloween store that takes over half a block of Westwood Blvd. My eye is drawn into the crowd. A face.

That face. Looking at me.

Jack.

As we lock looks, the light turns green. I can't move. Is it really him?

A car engine roars from around a corner. Marjan continues forward, chattering, rubbing her tired eyes. A souped-up Honda explodes from the corner into the intersection. People scream. I reel backward. Engine heat burns my ankles. The car strikes Marjan and one of the students. The student sprawls into the intersection, but Marjan is caught on the car grill. Her creamy chiffon blouse billows from her waist before she twists and slips onto the asphalt, crushed under the wheels.

I scream. And scream.

~

A massive block of decaying stone, Blarney Castle squatted under the cobalt sky. We climbed a twisted flight of thick, narrow steps in the southeast corner of the fortress. Sunlight angled through murder holes, painting bright stripes across the gray shell where an ancient fireplace hovered in the wall on the floorless second story. Once covered in filth, herbs, and sawdust, the castle's floors were now bare, the fortress itself a rugged husk. The jagged ruins of the battlements reminded me of Stonehenge as we reached the top.

"Time has carved memories into the stone," Jack mused as he perched on a ledge. He held out a thin white hand and helped me scramble up.

Bright green hills tumbled around the castle like rumpled blankets. Threads of darker green trees stitched the surface, running across the horizon to meet thick woods that clotted to the West. Like in the forests of Dr. Seuss, spindly trees with bristling purple heads twisted with whimsy in the sunlight. A variety of other trees spattered the landscape: evergreen and bushy, bright yellow-green and sparse. Nestled by a lake, an antiquated brick mansion with nine chimneys and long windows draped in white, waited for a master long dead. Through my camera's viewfinder, I noted a blue Citron parked by a servant's entrance.

Jack somberly gestured to the landscape. "My family lives there."

"Oh, really? In that mansion? Or the forest?" I raised a playful eyebrow. He'd told me at dinner the first night that he was a recent graduate of Aberdeen. The tour was a gift from his parents who lived in South Wales.

The stinging brightness of the sun punctuated his silence.

~

My boss texts me the news that evening that Marjan is alive but in a coma. The student is dead. No one got the license plate.

I call in sick the next morning and leave a voicemail for my therapist, requesting an appointment. I don't see her regularly, just when my family is being outrageous.

My cell phone rings. A number I don't recognize. Maybe it's about Lupa. I answer, hope lumping in my throat. "Hello?"

"Is this Nadya? This would be Mr. Peter McClatchy," the caller replies with a thick Irish brogue. "Mrs. McClatchy and I found yer dog."

Overjoyed, I hunt for a pen and paper. "Oh, thank goodness! Is she okay?"

"Aye, she's the spittin' image of good health. Mrs. McClatchy has been feedin' 'er a bit too well, I'm afraid."

"That's quite all right," I assure him. "I'm just grateful you found her and that you called."

"Not at all, not at all," the Irishman replied. "Now, will ya be wantin' to pick 'er up soon?"

"How about in an hour? Where are you located, Mr. McClatchy?"

"We're at the Irish shop on Highland and Wilshire. Y' can't miss it."

~

Windows blackened from inside, the Irish shop crouches between a pharmacy and a salsa dance studio in a strip mall. A passing bus throws sunlight against the dark glass, revealing a shamrock etched above the door.

"Oh, sure. You can't miss it...if you're James Bond." I clutch Lupa's folding chain leash as I shut the Kia door. I pull on the glass door's steel handle. A small bell *tinkles* above the opening.

Rows of shelves are crammed with imported crackers, five editions of Irish newspapers, Guinness swag, Riverdance videos, CDs, Celtic calendars and prayer books, crystal goblets and crosses, silver pens etched with saint names. I draw my shoulders together as I walk down the aisle for fear of sweeping items off the shelves. None of these trinkets reminds me of the sprawling emerald hills dotted with ancient manors, ruined and roofless in the mist.

The elderly Mr. McClatchy leans one elbow against the display case full of Claddagh rings and cross pendants, which doubles as a checkout stand with an antique-looking register. A red-checkered cabby hat slouches over his whitening hair that bristles around his ears and down a generous jaw. Not especially overweight, he is certainly not underfed himself. A silver tray of bagged homemade scones sits at his elbow. Slate blue eyes flicker when he notices me approaching the register.

"You must be Nadya." Mr. McClatchy grins so widely the back breach of his false teeth shows. He sticks his head through the doorway into the stockroom. "Sarah, will ya bring the dog, now?"

As we wait, my heart pounds, a geyser of love and excitement rumbling in my heart. My sweet, wonderful Lupa.

I tell Mr. McClatchy about my trip to Ireland earlier this year and the horrors of Aer Lingus. His eyes dance as he tells me of a time when they seated a 300-pound woman next to him on a flight. "She lifted the armrest and, Jesus and Mary, another hundred pounds fell down beside me."

Then Mr. McClatchy darkens. "Did ya hear about the two tourists who were murdered yesterday on the Santa Monica Pier?"

I hadn't. I was too busy living my own horror. I shake my head.

"This is a foul place that grows fouler every day, much in need of cleansing," he says. A wrinkled hand spattered in liver spots covers his mouth as his gaze settles somewhere beyond the store wall. "Sarah!" he yells. "What's keepin' ya?"

A wee woman emerges from the stockroom, rope in hand. I run around the glass counter to greet them.

My heart sinks as a black Labrador puppy turns the

corner of the doorway, tongue hanging happily from its slack coal jaws. Mrs. McClatchy proudly offers me the rope. "There she is, safe and sound," the old woman proclaims. Her raised brow draws a thin, sinister arc over the fog of her cataract.

"That's not my dog." I shake with anger. "They're not even the same color."

Mr. McClatchy steps toward me. "Ya'll take this dog," he hisses through his sallow teeth. "Fer Gwin-ap-neeth has yer hound and there'll be no gettin' 'er back without yer life. D'ya hear me? She belongs to the Lord of the Dead now."

Tears burning my eyes, I flee down the aisle, toppling stacked tins and bins. I yank open the door, bell jangling roughly, and jump into my Kia.

I have to retrieve the posters. Goddammit, I should have known there'd be freaks. I also feel guilty. Who knows where that puppy came from? Was it a stray? Abandoned? Lonely and scared? Would those people now discard it?

And where have I heard that name before? Gwin-ap-neeth? The Lord of the Dead? It sounds familiar.

Veils of golden sunlight spill from the parted clouds over the boulevard; the Kia squeals to a halt at the corner of Hollywood and Vista. As I tug the poster from the tree, something chilling catches my eye:

Doberman. Husky. Weimaraner. Labrador. German Shepherd. And more. On every palm tree and telephone pole flanking the boulevard flaps the poster for someone's lost dog.

He belongs to the Lord of the Dead now...

~

The last night in Dublin, Jack and I drank at the hotel bar. After two Irish coffees, I had exhausted my tales of being a creative director at an ad agency and the move to working in galleries. It was a big pay cut, but the gallery is much more relaxed. "So, you mentioned that Aberdeen required a dissertation for graduation. What was it about?"

Clearly delighted by my inquiry, Jack unraveled an utterly brilliant theory about retribution in our justice system having to do with enforced gift giving. He went on to describe the way many cultures use gift giving to enforce behavior and make allies. Our system of retribution, he argued, has not as much to do with replacing what was lost to society as it does with making the evildoer give a gift to those he has harmed. In some cases, his freedom. In others, his life.

His intellect roared like a bonfire and I was drawn to the flames. The way to my heart has always been through my mind. He found the way.

I told him excitedly about how, because my father is a Caucasian French national and my mother is African American, I got caught up in the immigration issues in France. But then I was asking myself, "Why are you so worked up about what's happening in your father's country of origin? Los Angeles has plenty of immigration issues and other social justice problems." So I brought it home. I started creating art installations about righting wrongs. It's been my passion. It's one reason I had to get out of the ad game. We were exploiting issues to sell a product. Maybe I could've stuck it out and worked from within, but it was sucking my life away. I marched with the half-million in downtown LA for the Dream Act. I worked with Otis College on a project to teach art to at-risk kids. I did whatever I could with my heart, with my words.

I paused when I saw Jack's face change from eager intellectual to a man awed. "You're a Gaul."

I laughed. "Yeah. Kind of." My dad would think that was very funny.

Jack downed the last of his Irish coffee and looked at me directly for the first time. "Would you like to go for a walk with me?"

We wandered down the streets of Temple Bar, our heads light with whiskey. Parades of tipsy bridal showers passed, celebrants wreathed in feather boas and crowned with plastic tiaras. Drunken couples groped and kissed in the street. Friends sang raucous songs out of key.

I shivered, burying my hands in my coat pockets, wondering how much of the cold was due to my thin blood. Jack held out his hand. I took it. Warm. Strong. Unexpectedly soft.

"A couple of the older women on the tour lectured me about leading you on. They said I was too old for you," I said.

Jack smiled demurely. "What did you tell them?"

"To mind their own fucking business."

He laughed. We then crested a hill overlooking the docks of Dublin. The street lamp streaked his fair skin with bluish light. Eyes staring intensely into mine, he took both of my hands and held them to his dry lips. I had thought about nothing but kissing them since we first met, and now I wanted to wet them every way possible.

"Once upon a time, there was a beautiful woman named Creiddyled," he began, "who was promised by King Arthur to a savage warrior named Gwythr. But Creiddyled loved the Lord of the Dead, whose other name was Gwynn ap Nudd." He pronounced the Lord's name gwin-ap-neeth. "He lived at the Otherworld gate of the Cliffs of Moher. On May night, after the wedding but before Gwythr's bed, Gwynn came for her with his wild pack of hell hounds to take her to the Otherworld."

"Sounds nauseatingly sexist," I replied.

"It was a different time. They didn't value women, or their strength. But I do. I believe Gwynn ap Nudd loved her for more than a bedmate. I believe he thought she'd

make an excellent leader of the Wild Hunt."

"A better leader in both heaven and hell, I'd wager." I grinned impishly.

His face glowed with happiness. And he kissed me.

~

Jack. It *can't* be. But if Jack is here and he has something to do with this, how is he involved? And why? I return to my apartment and do some research. I start with "Lord of the Dead" until I find information about Gwynn ap Nudd, as its spelling is so odd. Welsh. Jack had told me only half of a single variation on the story. Apparently Gwythr fought Gwynn ap Nudd at the Cliffs of Moher for Creiddyled's hand. It was a draw. They are to duel every May Day for her hand until Judgment Day. And every Hallows, Gwynn ap Nudd leads his hellhounds on a "hunt" to cleanse the land of evildoers.

The tour was just before May Day.

Now, it's "Hallows." Hallows Eve, anyway.

I need to go back to that store and get some answers.

~

Traffic clots as I approach Santa Monica Boulevard from the north. It's taken 45 minutes just to drive this far. While the infamous parade happens in West Hollywood, the general street party extends beyond Vine and as far north as Franklin. Fights erupt in the streets alongside dancing and drinking. Later tonight the police will cruise the area. But for now, I fight every inch of traffic to reach the Irish shop. Parking's much worse now that it's afternoon. The strip mall lot is packed. I circle around until a space opens up on the street three blocks away, just past the middle school. Before I reach the shop door, though, my heart drops into my shoes.

A heavy chain and lock secures two collapsible gates closed over the doorway.

"Nononono. This can't be."

I try to see inside the shop through the darkened glass, but to no avail.

"Hey, in there!" No answer. I run down the alley, around to the back of the building. The door to the shop is bolted shut. I bang on it. "Hey! You know why I'm here."

Nothing.

Anger burns back the tears as I head back to the sidewalk, heart heavy. Those bastards know something. They can't hide forever. I'll come back tomorrow. I'll bring friends. I slip my phone out of my purse, wondering whom to call. Police? Hell, my overbearing mother is enough to make anyone confess. Someone will make them explain if I can't.

A sniffling young man in ripped jeans and a leather jacket affixes a piece of paper to a telephone pole ahead of me. Lost dog. A white Pekinese.

Tears burn my cheeks. I'm so sorry. I know how you feel...

A scream.

I scan the area. A bald man wearing a dull green T-shirt and jeans stands in the street. He grips a handgun. Another is tucked in his waist. I don't think he sees me, but he's headed this way.

Shit.

I dive behind a curbed Prius and huddle against the wheel, clutching my purse to my chest.

A shot rings out.

More screams.

The young man drops to the ground next to me behind a motorcycle parked in front of the telephone pole. The bike offers him scant protection from a stray bullet. He's just a few feet away.

Sirens wail in the distance.

An explosion of glass.

More screams.

The bald man shouts, "She shouldn't have left me. She took the kids."

Two more shots.

Deafening.

Someone wails with grief.

Faintly, the school alarms ring down the block. Lockdown. Those poor babies.

The young man breathes heavily, eyes red. He might be having a panic attack.

Hang in there. Don't move.

"Goddamn bitch! Why'd she do that?"

The gunman is close. He radiates death.

My thighs, feet and low back shriek with pain. I hold tight against the car. Head down. My knuckles whiten around my cell phone.

"WHAT?"

Someone talks to the gunman from a window. Distracting him. The cacophony filters from up Highland. Police vehicles, radios, emergency crews. But I'm focused on the gunman's responses to the man up in the window.

"Did you hear me?" he shouts. "IF I HAVE TO SUFFER, YOU ALL SUFFER."

"Police! Drop your weapon. Hands above your head."

The young man behind the bike looks at me, beseeching.

The gunman steps closer. I can see in the reflection of the storefront glass the gunman's head turning this way and that, looking for potential targets. He doesn't seem to realize we're here. Ignoring the cops, he continues toward the school.

The young man makes a break to join me behind the car.

But just as he moves, my cell phone rings. Caller ID lights up. My therapist. I crush the button to silence the phone.

Too late.

Bullets rip into the young man behind the bike until he sprawls on the sidewalk in pools of blood.

And then a louder shot rings out.

Sniper.

~

We kissed in the hallway by my hotel room door. Although I ached for him, Jack refused my bed. "I'll see you again."

The next morning, as I boarded the coach headed to the airport, I grilled our tour guide, Paddy. "Where's Jack?"

"Who?" Paddy held his hand to his ear, mouth open quizzically.

"Jack O'Malley. The guy I was hanging out with. Where is he?"

Mouth full of tobacco-stained teeth, Paddy chuckled the way he did whenever I had asked to stop and photograph a graveyard or a standing stone (things so ridiculously common in Ireland, he didn't understand my fascination). "If he didn't tell ya, I surely can't," Paddy said, patting me on the shoulder. He winked. "Company policy."

~

My apartment is silent. I'm curled on the couch. Numb. Staring at Lupa's leash snaking across the coffee table. Lupa, my protector. My best friend. The ambulance crewmember said I was in acute stress. Depressed. Detached. It couldn't have been real. The shooting. The death. But these things happen in Los Angeles. They happen everywhere.

I want my dog back. The only soul in the world who can comfort me.

A thicker coat doesn't keep the icy air from mincing my bones. Leash in hand, I shuffle up to Runyon Canyon. It's dark, but everyone is alive with Halloween. Cocktail parties on house patios. Cars honking.

The gate to the dog park is ajar. I go in.

"Lost dog" posters cover every tree. Labs. Dobermans. Boston terriers. Mutts. Emotions overwhelm me as I climb higher. The loss of each pet. The grieving. We've lost our best friends. Each of us. Lost.

Damned.

The leash drags in the dirt. "Lupa! Where are you?" I break down, sobbing. I reach Inspiration Point and stop at the precipice, surveying the city lights sprawling beyond. "I love you, Lupa," I whisper.

Flashes of memory. Bullets tearing into that young man. Marjan's blouse billowing.

The mysterious bells chime in the copse of trees, just as before. Otherwordly. A flurry of shadows in the eucalyptus branches. A squall abruptly slaps my face.

I turn to face the woods.

Breaking from the copse, they run toward me. Tongues blackened. Eyes burning. Doberman. Husky. Weimaraner. Labrador. German Shepherd...

Wolf.

Lupa.

I fall to my knees. She joyously licks my face, her golden eyes shining. Molten. Her fur smells of pine and dirt. The rapture of being reunited with Lupa consumes me, but there's something behind her.

A black stallion emerges from the copse. The fog of the steed's breath curls white in the darkness as it paws the ground like the Nightmare in Fuseli's painting. On its back, a rider.

Jack.

He slides from the horse's back, landing on the ground

with a thunderclap. Lupa barks. When he lowers himself to one knee, she races to him, licking his hands and face.

"What the hell are you doing with my dog?" I yell. "And what the fuck are you doing here? Are you following me? A fucking international stalker?"

He wears a black T-shirt and jeans, black sneakers with a death's head painted on the canvas. His bangs are slicked up in front like a pop star. Who the hell is this guy?

And then I know.

He answers. Voice lyrical. "I told you we'd meet again." His eyes faintly shine like Lupa's.

I'm overheating with rage. "Is this some kind of fucking romantic gesture? Stealing my dog and returning him? Seriously?" I'm also shaking. "Who are you really?"

He shakes his head. "You know who I am."

The dogs surround him, sitting obediently. Tails wagging. Panting. Looking expectantly at their master. Dogs I've seen in the posters. Dogs I don't recognize at all. I imagine the terrible pain their owners must feel.

"Whatever it is, I'm not into it. Do you know what I've been through today?"

"I do. I'm sorry. I had to show you how much you're needed."

"For what? PTSD experiments?"

"Remember when I said that I believed Gwynn ap Nudd thought Creiddyled would make an excellent leader of the Wild Hunt?"

Jack steps closer, that sweet face imploring. The anger. The terror. Everything melts away, leaving a peace. A strange feeling of satisfaction. Even a pang in my heart.

"Look. The police did a damned good job of 'cleansing' today, okay? They don't need some vigilante Goth to help."

"What about your friend, Marjan? Or the tourists on the pier?"

I couldn't answer.

"I wasn't on the tour to woo you, Nadya. I was searching for someone to lead The Hunt here. A woman with keen intelligence. Deep feeling. A tireless sense of justice." He blinks sadly. "That I loved you was beside the point. And still is. But I need you. You've seen that the last few days."

"I just want my dog back," I say. "Lupa! Come here, girl."

She doesn't budge.

"LUPA."

"She won't come. Only if you ride Rhiannon." He unwraps the stallion's reins from his hand and offers them to me. "Then you can be reunited. In heart. And even purpose."

Lupa whines, giving me her "Let's go outside and play" look. It breaks my heart.

"You're an asshole," I say to Jack.

"Look," Jack says. "You can trust me. You know how wolves are. If I wasn't trustworthy, Lupa wouldn't have answered me."

He's right. Lupa seems to truly adore him. "Even if I did trust you, I don't understand what you're asking. Are you really Gwynn ap Nudd? That's just a fairy tale."

"I'm asking you to accept your destiny." He offers the reins again.

Destiny. I sense a power older than the Cliffs themselves in those reins. The horse's eyes reflect a stillness and beauty I have only ever seen in great art. Perhaps this—whatever it is—is my destiny. Or perhaps I simply love Lupa more than anything in the world.

It's funny how love and destiny feel the same.

The moment I take the reins, the dogs crowd around me, howling with joy. There's nothing like a happy dog. And here's at least a hundred of them.

The power of the reins surges into my body, wave after wave. Courage profound. Strength frightening. With a new instinct, I stroke Rhiannon's nose and deftly mount her from the left. On her back, I survey Los Angeles from the Point with new eyes. What were once buildings and houses now erupt into flames throughout the landscape. I feel drawn to each one, rage and revenge boiling my blood.

"You see the fires?" Jack asks. "A terrible evil is happening at each one. An innocent is being harmed."

"So what do I do?"

"You'll harvest the flames. The hounds know what to do."

A hundred or so dogs leap, bark and wag their tails as they crowd about my heels. They seem eager to get to the fires. But I can't do this. They're not my dogs. I think about the black puppy Mrs. McClatchy held on the rope. So many abandoned and unloved...

"Go," I tell the dogs. "Return to your human families."

The dogs pour down the park hillside. Running home.

Jack's eyes flash with fury. "What have you done? You can't hunt without your hounds!"

"You're right. Heel, Lupa." Holding the reins in my left hand, I squeeze the horse with my knees. "Rhiannon—*ride*."

And we do. Into the alleyways. Through the parks. Parking lots, underpasses and streets. To the edges of Los Angeles County and beyond. As we gallop, Lupa at our heels, new dogs join us. The abandoned, the hungry, the forgotten. The unloved. That adorable black puppy, which the bastard McClatchys had taken back to the shelter. They will have a "forever home" every time we return to the Underworld. Those dogs are part of my eternal pack.

My Hunt.

And the Cleansing begins.

THE PATCH

By Eric Miller

"The pumpkin screamed."

Billy barely heard Caroline over the talk radio host yammering out of the boom box sitting on his cluttered workbench. He was bent over the engine of his '63 Impala, trying to make sense of a jumble of greasy spark plug wires.

"The pumpkin did what?" he asked.

"It screamed," she said softly.

Something in her voice made Billy look up. He leaned around the hood and saw his wife standing in the doorway to the house, her face pale and lips trembling. He grabbed a shop towel and wiped his hands as he walked over to her, instinctively moving slowly; she looked like a frightened horse ready to bolt.

He smiled and spoke soothingly. "It's okay, Caroline. Everything is all right. Just start over and tell me what's going on."

She took a deep breath. "I was in the kitchen, getting ready to carve the pumpkin for the Jack-O-Lantern. I covered the table in paper so it wouldn't make a mess like last year. I was going to cut around the top, so I could—"

Her voice cracked.

Billy grabbed her hands and steadied her. "So you could scoop the guts and seeds out, right. Go on."

After a moment she continued. "I got out the knife and

sharpened it and then got ready to carve it. But when I stuck it in..."

Tears burst out of her eyes and spilled down her cheeks. He held her tight as she sobbed.

"Oh God, Billy. I've never heard anything that awful in my whole life..."

~

Billy stepped into the kitchen. Caroline had stayed right behind him all the way from the garage, but she stopped in the dining room doorway and wouldn't move another inch.

He looked around the room and saw a completely normal mid-west kitchen; a sink half-full of dirty dishes, bowls of Halloween candy on the counter, a pot of beef stew simmering on the stove—and in the middle of it all on the square table covered in newspapers sat a fat round pumpkin with a carving knife sticking out of the top.

Billy looked back at his wife. His first inclination had been that she was pulling a big joke on him, but she wasn't the joking type. Still, everyone knew plants didn't scream. She had probably heard some kids outside playing *The Walking Dead*, or the show itself on the TV. But the TV was, off, and the double-paned windows he put in last fall for insulation and sound proofing were closed. And she was clearly petrified of *something*.

He smiled and pointed to the table. "Is that it?"

She nodded.

"All right. I'm going to check it out." He started to walk closer, but she grabbed his arm and held him back.

"Be careful..." she pleaded.

"Always am."

Billy gently pulled his arm away and walked over to the kitchen table. In the overhead light he thought the pumpkin looked completely, one hundred percent normal. A fat orange globe with a knife stuck half way in, a fruit or vegetable or whatever the hell it was, an hour away from having a scary face carved into it and a candle stuck inside. Tomorrow night for Halloween it would be put on the front porch to scare the trick-or-treaters.

Once again he got the feeling he was the butt of some massive joke, or maybe even on one of those stupid reality TV shows where they scared people for "fun," but one look back at Caroline's haunted eyes and he knew that whatever this was, whatever she had heard, it was real. So he walked up to the table, put both hands on either side of the pumpkin and screwed up his courage.

"All right, pumpkin, this is what is going to happen. I'm going to cut your top off, clean you out and carve a big happy face on you so we can all laugh about this tomorrow. And we might even make a pie out of you, too. So I'd appreciate it if you'd just keep quiet long enough for me to do the job."

The pumpkin didn't answer.

Billy reached out for the knife, but when he almost touched the white handle, he pulled his hand back. He laughed at himself, then smiled back over his shoulder. "You got me a little jumpy, sweetie."

She didn't smile back. "Stop joking around, Billy."

He nodded and turned back to the table, more serious this time. He reached out and grabbed the gnarled stalk with one hand and the knife handle with the other. He took a deep breath and pulled the blade free.

And the pumpkin screeched in soul-searing agony.

Billy jerked his hand off the pumpkin stalk, spinning the gourd around on the table. He dropped the knife without thinking, and he and Caroline found themselves in the other room before they even knew they had moved.

Billy was shaking. "Holy hell, you weren't kidding! What *was* that?"

"I don't know, I just don't know!" she said.

Billy cautiously leaned around the door sill, peeking back into the kitchen. The pumpkin had rolled on its side and the blade lay on the floor where he had dropped it. He thought it was silent, but when he listened closer, he could hear it sobbing quietly. He turned around and went back to Caroline.

"This is freaking crazy. We have to call the police." She said.

"Oh, right, and tell them what? They probably get a hundred prank calls a night this time of year. They'd either arrest us or throw us in the nut house."

"Then what do we do?"

"I don't know, but we're sure the hell aren't going to stab it anymore."

They collapsed on the couch and hugged each other tight. Billy rocked her in his arms as she cried, and had a hard time fighting back tears himself.

"Where the hell did you buy it, anyway? The grocery? Some farm stand?" He asked.

Caroline didn't answer.

Billy pulled back and looked her in the eye. "Where did you get it?"

She answered timidly. "From the back yard."

"We don't have a pumpkin patch in the back yard."

"We don't, but Mr. Hansen does."

Billy glared at her. "I told you to stay away from that guy. There's something wrong with him."

"I did. I swear. But you know his field—it's overgrown with all kinds of things. And when I was cutting the grass last week I saw a big pumpkin vine curling up the fence. The pumpkin was just on our side, and it looked so perfect. I figured I could save a trip to the store and he would never know…"

"Show me."

~

Billy's flashlight lit the way through the back yard, past the storage shed and into the weed-covered field beyond. Their property was only an acre, the last house in town, surrounded on the back three sides by a rusty fence. But the yard next door—the field behind Mr. Hansen's farmhouse—stretched for a hundred acres or more, a mile back from the fence to the clump of trees that surrounded his dilapidated house and sagging barn.

Billy stumbled in an unseen gopher hole and cursed, then led the way to the fence. Caroline stayed behind him the whole way. At the very back, he shined the light and saw the vine Caroline had told him about. It was thick, thicker than any he had ever seen before, a green-grey tangle of growth leading into the thick brush of Hansen's field. He traced the vine with the light to where it hung over the fence, to where the stalk had obviously been cut. He leaned forward to examine the end, and saw a reddish fluid had oozed out of it and dried. It almost looked like...

"Is that blood?"

Billy jumped at Caroline's voice. He had been thinking the exact same thing, but couldn't admit it to her. "I—No. I don't know what it is. But it isn't right."

"What are we going to do now?"

He motioned towards the Hansen house. "I'm going to go over there and find out what he's growing."

"Not tonight. Not in the dark."

Billy looked across the field at the Hansen house, sitting for all the world like a ghostly mansion in the middle of a haunted forest. He realized she was right.

"Good idea. I'll go over there tomorrow morning and get this sorted out."

"What about the pumpkin?"

"Leave it for tonight. Now come on, let's pack a bag and get the hell out of here. No way are we sleeping in the same house with that thing."

~

The Holiday Inn out on Highway 50 had seen better days, but to Billy and Caroline it was heaven. They took a long hot shower together, the first time they had done so in years, and by the time they got to bed, they were laughing about the incident.

"I don't think I saw you run that fast since high school football."

"Me? You were halfway out the front door by the time I dropped the knife!"

They laughed away the nerves for a while, then the serious mood dropped back over them. Caroline snuggled up in her husband's protective arms.

"What are we going to do with it?"

"I'm going to put it in a trash sack and take it back to Mr. Hansen. I don't care what he does with the damn thing as long as I never have to hear it again. Then everything will be all right."

"Are you sure?"

"It'll all look better in the daylight."

Caroline finally fell asleep at about three in the morning, but Billy stayed awake the whole time, staring at the shadows on the ceiling and turning the plan over and over in his mind. He left early, right after dawn, leaving Caroline sleeping.

~

Billy drove back to the house, went straight to the garage, and found the thickest work gloves he owned. He put them on, grabbed a sturdy cardboard box, and went into the kitchen.

As it turned out, he was wrong.

It didn't look better in the daylight.

The pumpkin had oozed red fluid all over the floor, a

thick, bloody sap that smelled like rotten vegetables and at the same time had a coppery tang. Billy was a hunter, and had cleaned enough game to know what blood smelled like. This was almost the same, but somehow horrifyingly different. He put it out his mind and picked the thing up, closing it in the box as fast as he could.

He vowed to himself that after he took the box to Hansen's, he would stop off at the Pantry and get a gallon of bleach to clean the floor. Two gallons, just to be sure.

~

The sagging front porch squeaked loudly as Billy walked to Mr. Hansen's front door and knocked. While waiting for an answer, he stepped back and looked at the house. The place was at least a hundred years old, a hulking farm house sliding more to ruin every year, the paint chipping off to reveal aged grey wood siding underneath. There was a sense of faded grandeur about the place to be sure, but to Billy, on Halloween day, with a few hours fitful sleep and a screaming pumpkin in a box under his arm, it looked downright evil.

And then there was Mr. Hansen himself. The man had been rude to them from the first time they met. When Caroline had brought over some freshly baked muffins as her way of saying "hi," he barely opened the door, and though he took a muffin, he made a big show of spitting out the first bite and accusing Caroline of trying to poison him.

After that, it was an endless series of disputes over the fence line, Hansen angry over their dog Ollie running around his field, the man making loud (and odd) noises at all hours of the night, and just general strange looks and behavior. And while Billy couldn't prove it, he was certain Mr. Hansen had run over Ollie on purpose the year before. Ollie lived, but the operation to fix his broken legs cost a fortune, and in the end Billy had sent the dog away to live with his brother in Ft. Wayne rather than give his vile neighbor a chance to finish the job.

Rumors around town were that Mr. Hansen was the last of a long line of witches and warlocks, the house was haunted, and evil doings had been going on out at the farm since before the town had been founded. Billy didn't put much stock in any of this. Until the pumpkin, he didn't believe in anything supernatural, and even now he was sure there was some rational explanation for everything. To him, Mr. Hansen was just an old, crazy asshole, and someone he was finally going to have a showdown with.

He knocked again, louder, angry at being ignored.

There was still no answer.

Billy gave up, and walked around the side of the house to the driveway. He followed it behind the house. The back yard was as overgrown as the front. The fields were lorded over by an ancient, gnarled tree whose leaves had already fallen. The skeletal form looked right at home.

Billy started to knock on the back door, then heard a sound from behind him. He turned and looked at the open barn doors, and thought he saw movement. He walked in that direction.

Mr. Hansen stepped out of the barn and blocked the doorway. The light from inside flickered as if from a lantern or candles. He looked back at Hansen, expecting to see the usual red-faced fury on the man, but instead saw a look of amusement. And he noticed another thing about the farmer. For the life of him, Billy couldn't tell Hansen's age. In previous encounters he had thought the man was ancient and shriveled, but now he looked young and spry. The deep lines on his face had softened. Or had it just been dirt from the fields? How old *was* the guy?

Hansen's voice broke Billy's reverie. "You're trespassing."

Bill shook his head. "Sorry. I knocked at the house, but

no one answered."

"How could I? I was in the barn. Now what do you want?"

"I've got something here you might know about. We got it from one of your vines."

"You stole from me?"

"We didn't steal anything. Your vines were growing over our fence, and we took it from our side. That makes it ours. And it was just a pumpkin."

"A pumpkin?" Hansen got a weird gleam in his eye.

"Yes, a pumpkin. And there's something strange about it."

"Nothing strange about a pumpkin."

"There is about this one. It screams."

Hansen glared at him for a long moment. Then: "You're crazy, boy. Pumpkins don't make sounds."

"I said the same thing yesterday, but here we are."

"Let's hear it then. Get your trick or treat joke over with and leave me be."

Billy sat the box on the ground and bent down to open the top. He gingerly grabbed the orange gourd and pulled it out. "Maybe you can tell me what the hell you are growing over—"

Billy looked up and saw that Mr. Hansen was gone. The man's absence revealed the open barn door, and what was inside the crumbling structure: Candles sat everywhere in the gloomy building, shining down on the floor and illuminating a pentagram traced sloppily in blood. A decapitated goat's head was in the middle of the demonic star and a large upside-down cross hung from a rafter.

Realization slammed into Billy's brain at the sight; all the old stories were true. Hansen was some kind of demon worshipper, or a demon himself. It explained all the strange behavior and indeed, the screaming pumpkin.

He saw something out of the corner of his eye and turned to see the familiar old angry Hansen lunging towards him. The farmer brought a shovel down on top of Billy's head with a cartoon "splang."

Billy and the pumpkin dropped to the ground.

Everything faded to darkness.

~

The roaring headache was the first thing Billy was aware of. The next thing was that he couldn't move. As he wiggled around he figured out why; he was buried in dirt up to his neck, leaving only his head exposed. He blinked soil out of his eyes and tried to look around, but found he was at the bottom of a small pit and he couldn't see over the earthen rim.

"Help!" he yelled, thought the effort made his head pound harder and he almost blacked out again. He opened his mouth to yell again and a clod of dirt rolled onto his tongue. He choked and gagged trying to spit it out.

Mr. Hansen appeared over the pit, the shovel in his hand. "You're awake then," he said matter-of-factly.

"No thanks to you," Billy replied angrily. "Now get me out of here."

"Too late. You're planted."

"Planted!? What the hell are you talking about?"

"You wanted to know what kind of crops I was growing in my patch, and now you're going to find out."

Hansen got down on his knees and leaned over the small pit. He opened a rough hand so Billy could see what he held; a pumpkin seed.

"Open up."

Billy growled through clenched teeth. "The hell with you."

"Have it your way." Hansen grabbed the shovel and moved the sharp tip towards Billy's mouth.

Visions of splintered, bloody teeth made Billy scream "No!"

Hansen quickly popped the seed in Billy's open mouth, then slapped a length of tape over his lips before Billy could spit it out.

Billy snapped his head back and forth in panic, trying to dislodge the tape and somehow get free of the nightmare, but all he managed to do was knock more soil into his eyes. He looked up to see Mr. Hansen had gotten to his feet and scooped up a shovel full of dirt.

"MMMMFF!! FFFFGHHH!!" Billy raged.

Hansen smiled down at him and dumped the earth over Billy's head. "Happy Halloween."

"Masks beneath masks until suddenly the bare bloodless skull."
—Salman Rushdie, *The Satanic Verses*

BENEATH IT ALL

By E.S. Magill

Autumn finally arrives at the end of September. Summer relents, and Persephone makes her journey to the Underworld. Francine has already packed her summer clothes, placed them in storage bins stowed away at the back of her closet. Tank tops and strappy sandals exposing as much flesh as possible to summer sun are folded away to be replaced by leather and wool. Like Demeter, Francine cannot stop the inevitable—only make the best of the situation. She pulls on leggings and boots. She dresses in a skirt, a turtleneck, a blouse, a scarf, and a knee-length sweater—as if layers can shield her from the world. When she ambles into work, her colleagues, at their desks or standing about, look. She deposits her insulated lunch bag in the break room's fridge. As she heads for her office she greets everyone with a smile or a cheerful quip. It is a Friday, and at the end of the day she leaves for her vacation as she does every year. Her version of exile from the world.

Her office door is ajar.

She remembered locking it as she left yesterday. The custodian must have forgotten after making his rounds last night. Francine pushes the door open. She stops, hand still on the knob. She can go no further, trapped in the doorway. Her desk is kept meticulously neat. Papers stored out of sight in files in drawers. Books on their shelves. The only items on her desk are a computer monitor, a stapler, a tape dispenser, a pencil holder, and her name plate: Francine D. Williams. The thing sitting in the middle of the antimicrobial desk pad does not belong.

Any other time of the year it would have been innocuous, but someone has left it with intent, benign or otherwise. Francine sees it as a harbinger of what is to come.

Her shoulders tremble. Sweat lines her upper lip. Her legs nothing more than pipe cleaners barely keeping her upright. But she breathes as she was taught to do in these situations—in through her nose and out through her mouth. This keeps her from hyperventilating and passing out. Despite the terror strumming every nerve in her body, her brain is at work plowing through all the cautionary steps she took to avoid something like this: letting colleagues know of her condition, leaving the office for a month, remembering to take her medications every morning.

Vacation begins when she leaves at four o'clock today. Her suitcases are packed. Boxes of canned food, tea, coffee, spices wait next to the suitcases. Did she pack the baking powder and soda? Another box holds books and DVDs—because the internet is not reliable where she is going.

It is too early, October 1st still several days away. If this had happened on Monday she would not have been here. She planned her vacation so she would have an entire month to avoid something like this. Every year it seemed to come earlier and earlier.

"Happy Halloween, Franny! Like your surprise? I wanted you to have it before you left today." Meyer beams rays of puerile glee.

Words are locked in her throat. Her fingers grip the handle of her briefcase. Nails dig furrows into her palms. The light trench coat, judiciously remembered in the event of rain now that it is autumn, slips off her arm. The cascading fabric sounds like the rustle of windblown leaves.

Meyer picks it up for her, tries to hand it back.

She cannot extend her arm.

"You don't have to stand there in such awe. It's just a little something I put together to say thank you." When she says nothing, his face transforms into that dog-done-something-bad look. "Oh, hey. Are you on a diet? I mean you don't need to be on a diet because you look great all the time." When she doesn't respond, he stammers on. "Oh no, do you belong to one of those religions that doesn't celebrate Halloween?"

"Get out of the way." Patty appears and elbows the man aside. "Christsakes, October doesn't even start until next week, Meyer," she says.

Patty is Francine's friend, a work friend, but besides office happy hours, they have gone to the movies together, shopped. "What's the fuckhead done now, sweety?"

Francine can only stare.

Patty follows her gaze. She steps around Francine and advances to the desk. She deposits the Halloween item into the trash.

"Oh, come on." Meyer continues his yammering. "This is stupid. All this over that? I don't believe it."

Patty takes the can and shoves it into Meyer's hands.

"No way! It's just candy. It's not like I left a live spider on her desk."

She pulls Francine into the office and shuts the door on Meyer.

~

"I'm not going to wear it!"

"Franny, it's just a costume. Everyone at the party will be wearing costumes."

It is Halloween, and Francine is six-years-old. She wedges her body further under the bed until her back touches the wall. Nothing clutters the space beneath Francine's bed—no books, no stray shoe, not even dust.

Her mother lifts the bed skirt. She holds the mask and costume in her hands. It lies limp like a shed skin. Francine shuts her eyes and turns her head away.

"It's not scary, just a pretty costume—a fairy princess with wings, a tiara, a wand. See?" Her mother holds each piece out to her for inspection.

Francine will not look.

"Is it the mask?" Her mother strokes its feathers. "It's just for your eyes. Remember when I brought it back from New Orleans? You thought it was beautiful." Her mother stretches her arm under the bed, the mask delicately clutched between fingers and thumb.

Francine screams.

"Geezus, what the hell is going on in here?" Francine's father enters her bedroom. She can only see his shiny black shoes.

Her mother lowers the bed skirt and sits back on her knees. "She won't come out. She doesn't want to wear the costume."

"You mean she'd rather go as something else? We could rustle something up for her to wear, but we need to get going."

"No, she's afraid of costumes," her mother says.

He looks skeptically at the fairy princess ensemble.

Her mother shrugs. "I've told her it's harmless, but she won't believe me."

"Look," he says to his wife, "why don't you get your costume on. It's late, and you know how my boss feels about tardiness. I'll reason with her."

Her father lifts the bed skirt. He is dressed as Count Dracula—slicked back hair, pale face, fangs, black cape. He holds a hand out to her. "Come on, baby. Come out, and we can discuss this."

Francine's eyes grow huge at the sight of him. "No,

Daddy. Don't wear that. Take it off!" Her voice comes out knifelike, a blade just sharpened.

"God, Franny, the neighbors are going to think we're killing you."

"Take it off, Daddy. They'll find you. If you wear the costume, they'll find you." Francine pulls the collar of her shirt up and wipes her dripping nose.

"Who's going to find me?"

"They'll find you. Don't pretend, Daddy." She has cried so much her voice comes out in hitches, like going over speed bumps.

"I have no idea what you're talking about Francine Williams. You are being completely irrational. You listen to me: There are no they, no boogeymen, no monsters. This is a costume. We're playing pretend. Do you understand what I'm saying?"

Francine doesn't know what irrational means, but from her father's tone she knows he doesn't believe her. But he has to. She understands. She has to make him understand too. "If you put the costume on, it's easier for them to see you and find you. You won't be you anymore."

Her father stares at her trying to process what she has told him. "This is ridiculous. Daddy isn't going to become a vampire. People don't turn into their costumes. Costumes are for fun, only." He plops down on his stomach and reaches for her. His fingers like tentacles stretch toward her.

Francine screams and pushes against the wall, but it is as far as she can go.

Her father hooks a finger into her T-shirt and drags her toward him. The vampire face hangs like a full moon at the edge of her bed, becoming larger with each tug. The fangs protrude from his mouth, biting into his lower lip.

Francine kicks and digs her fingers into the carpet for purchase.

"Martin, you are scaring her to death." Francine can see her mother's shoes. They have heels like the long nails her father uses in his workshop.

Francine's head emerges first. The woman in the room with the vampire is dressed in a black dress and perched on her head is a witch's hat.

They will come now. They will come and find them.

Francine's eyes roll back in their sockets and her body convulses.

~

The morning sun hovers at the edge of the lake. Every day Francine takes her first cup of coffee on the front porch of the cabin. She folds her legs under her bottom and tucks her robe around her bare skin against the morning chill. Steam swirls up from her coffee in a fragrant spiral. From across the lake, geese call out. She is ten miles from the nearest town, a burg of several thousand people. She has never been to it. Her vacation is spent in a cabin at the edge of a lake, surrounded by a forest. It can only be reached down a rutted dirt road. For the first year it was a just a week, several years later two, now she enjoys the entire month. She knows what she will find if she goes into town— what is everywhere across the U.S. at this time of year and has migrated to other countries as well. She shakes her head as if thoughts are sand that can be scattered.

After morning chores, Francine heads out for a hike around the lake. Over her jacket she wears a bright orange vest. Public lands surround the cabin, and it is hunting season for a lucky few who can get the special permits. Along her walk she collects leaves—sweetgum and sycamore—for a Thanksgiving table-scape project. The air still holds the morning chill, but she finds it delicious, reminiscent of apple cider and sugar cookies. She finds it ironic that she can still enjoy this time of year while coping with her debilitating phobia, like two paths, light and dark, paralleling each other—one too terrifying for her to walk. With therapy and pharmacology she grasps the irrationality of what she believes about Halloween. She tells herself it isn't real, just her brain playing tricks on her. Still, she can't understand the pleasure people derive from images of skulls and monsters and haunted houses. Being frightened is not an emotion she seeks out. But the worst part is the costumes and masks people casually wear without a thought of what can happen to them. All the Halloween props are signals for them to come, a welcoming.

She is obsessing and missing out on the pleasure of the hike. She changes gears and starts thinking it might be nice to get a dog. It would walk at her side, keep her company. Or a cat—not black though—waiting for her at home by the hearth.

The walk warms her, and she unzips her jacket. Perhaps she should just move here. Accounting doesn't need an office. The cabin's owner is getting on in years and has admitted to no longer using the place as often as she once did. Francine knows she can convince the woman to sell.

Francine stops and turns to the lake. The water laps at the shore, tasting the pebbles and mud there. A fish leaps in the distance, a silver ribbon. She has thought all this before, moving to this place where she can control her surroundings. Back at the cabin there is a box with magazines and clippings of decorating ideas she has collected through the years. It serves as her version of a hope chest.

The rifle shot thunders across the lake. For a few seconds, it displaces all other sounds. Francine drops to her knees and hunkers down to wait. Hunters are supposed to avoid the cabin. Though the shot wasn't directed at her, she bristles at the thought of someone violating her space. She pops her head up and looks around. Across the lake, she spots a figure standing at the water's edge. He is too distant to make out his features, his face a smudge, but he stares in her direction. The figure turns and heads into the forest.

~

"So explain it to me again, please. You hate Halloween, but why is it you particularly fear masks and costumes?"

The walls of the psychiatrist's office are white and bare. No paintings of serene seascapes to sooth agitated minds. No plants. No bookcases—in fact, not a book in sight. No family portrait in a silver frame. Even the one window is covered with white blinds. There is nothing in this room for Francine to fix her eye on. She isn't even reclining upon a couch as she has seen in so many movies. Instead, she sits in a cheap office chair—its fabric seat threadbare and stained black—facing her doctor.

He is explaining to her that doesn't do talk therapy. His job is to listen and diagnose. If therapy is warranted, another person will fulfill that role. The doctor keeps his head down as he listens, scribbling notes and asking the occasional clarifying question. He will not reveal is eyes to her as he speaks.

Francine is thirteen-years-old. This year's incident at school finally forced a referral to a mental health profes-sional. Not so much for herself, but because she had fright-ened the other students in her English class when she kept screaming and screaming. The teacher thought a video of *The Legend of Sleepy Hollow* would be a fun way of kick-ing off October.

"So, Francine, if I were to put on a costume right now, what would be your reaction?"

Her heart beats faster. "Please don't. They—they might find you and force you to become—to become it—the costume." At her age, Francine knows she sounds crazy. She finds it difficult to convince others of what she knows to be true. Her ideas rejected by everyone—her parents, teachers, friends, doctors.

"I have a question for you, Francine. Here me out: What if people wear masks and costumes to reveal their true inner self?"

Her head snaps back as if the psychiatrist has reached across his desk and slapped her. This idea balloons up in her mind.

"Do you know that's a conventional thought, Francine?" The doctor leans back in his chair. "Ask most people why they have chosen a particular costume and they'll probably tell you that it reveals some hidden character trait. If a person dresses as a serial killer from a slasher movie, perhaps he harbors violent thoughts. If someone dresses in a sexy costume, maybe deep down she wants to be more desired."

Francine grimaces.

"Just hear me out, Francine. Isn't that what you want from others: Just to be heard?"

She shrugs and nods for him to continue. Her stomach roils. She might be sick.

"What if the costume is the medium by which repressed desires are made manifest? You choose the costume because that's who you really are."

The doctor's words become a hollow ringing in her head. Soon she can't even understand him, his words all noise

"No. That's not how it works," she says. There is a pressure behind her eyeballs. "You put the costume on, and they find you and they force you to be that forever. They come for you. They only have one night a year to do this, Halloween. Why don't you believe me?" Francine is on her feet, shouting at the doctor.

The psychiatrist tries to maneuver her back into the chair.

Francine twists away from him. "They watch and wait. They come for you on that one night. Why won't you believe me?"

"Francine, I'm here to help you."

"No, you're not." She moves around to the back of her chair out of the doctor's reach. "If you want to help, then just believe me. Why can't you believe me?"

The doctor drops his arms to side. "Because your mind is deceiving you, Francine."

She grows still. Time ticks by, widening the gulf between patient and doctor. She now understands she will never convince him. In fact, she will never convince anyone about what she believes.

He helps her into the chair and returns to his own desk. Her chart will read *Paranoid. Delusional. Samhainophobia.*

~

"Can you afford not to go back to work?" Patty asks.

For the past four years Patty drives up to visit Francine for a weekend of Francine's vacation. The two women are sitting on the deck overlooking the lake and eating the pizza Patty always picks up on her way to the cabin. The sun sets. The last rays reflect off the white wine in her glass. Francine likes the sparkle it creates. She imagines she is drinking stars.

"Yeah, I can manage it. I'm just tired of being scared all the time," Francine says. "I never know when that first trigger is going to happen. I control things here."

Patty sets down her glass and looks seriously at her friend. "The meds don't help?"

"Sure they do. If they didn't, I would break down a lot sooner than I usually do. Hell, we couldn't even have this conversation if I weren't medicated."

"Yeah, I know," Patty says. She turns quiet and stares off across the lake.

Francine senses the shift in her friend's mood. "What's wrong?"

A minute passes before Patty speaks. "Do you really believe it, that costumes and masks can turn people?"

"No, it's not like that. It's not the props; it's them. They come and turn you."

Patty inches forward in her chair and crosses her arms across her chest. She scrutinizes her friend. "You know I love you, girl? And any other time of the year, you're a blast to be around, but right now..." Patty shrugs and shakes her head. "You know I dress up, go to Halloween parties?"

"Patty!"

"Don't judge, Franny. That's what people do—the costumes, parties."

Francine laughs. "Normal people. Not crazy, delusional people."

"Don't say that about yourself, Franny."

"Why not? Everyone thinks it. I can't help what I believe, Patty."

"And we believe something too. Have you ever thought about that? It's just pretend. Halloween and the costumes allow people to escape their mundane lives for a few hours. People what to experience the exotic, something outside of themselves."

Francine knows she can't convince her friend. No one has ever believed her.

"You're not coming back, are you?" Patty asks.

Francine remains silent for a moment. Her answer will determine everything. Before she can answer, Patty sits up and looks around Francine.

"Who's that over there?"

Francine turns around to see where her friend is looking. A shadow disappears into the forest.

~

It had only been a college Halloween prank.

Her friends hold Francine down, laughing as they do it. They pull the mask, white and featureless, over her face.

Later she wakes in a hospital. Her throat is raw and burning. But in her head she still hears herself screaming.

~

"Do you know if there are any new cabins in the area?" she asks the grocery delivery man. Since Patty left, Francine has not ventured into the forest, keeping outdoor forays to the area surrounding the cabin.

"Nope. You're the only person out here." He hands her a computer tablet. Francine signs her name, and he wishes her a good day. She doesn't want him to go. The loneliness of the place has settled on her. She puts away the groceries and then goes outside to bring in wood.

"Hello!"

Francine looks up, thinking it is the delivery man returned.

A stranger is standing near the boat dock. He waves at her.

The logs she cradles in her arms prohibit her from returning the greeting. If she could have, it would have been only out of politeness. He is too close to the cabin. But he soon turns away and continues along the trail around the lake. Overhead the sky is sheeted with bruised clouds threatening rain.

Late afternoon a thunderstorm starts up. Francine stands at the kitchen window and watches the rain fall into the lake, muting the separation of earth and sky. She stares at the dock where the man had been standing. Even though it is too early, she prepares dinner. Afterward she builds a fire and sets a kettle of water on the stove for tea. It is a few days until the end of October, and the weather has turned cold, winter come early—as if Persephone has settled into her prison.

Francine curls up on the sofa to read. Thunder cracks, followed by lightning. The cabin's lights flicker. There is no generator. If the lights go out, she will be in the dark. She sets the book down and pads to the kitchen pantry. She finds the box of candles, matches, flashlights and batteries and carries it into the living room.

The lights flicker once more, then the room goes dark. Francine picks up a flashlight and turns it on. Its light projects onto a window across the room. A man is staring in at her.

~

Halloween day has arrived. Francine sits huddled on the sofa—has turned it into a bed in fact. The doors to the two bedrooms are nailed shut. She has done the same to the front door. The back one is a sliding glass door leading out to the deck. Without going outside and nailing a sheet of plywood over it, there is no way to insure its integrity. Instead she has drawn its vertical blinds—has drawn the blinds on all the windows. Since the storm, since she saw the man at the window, she has remained within the confines of the cabin.

They have always been waiting for her. But why? She has never participated in the rituals of Halloween. She's never worn a costume or donned a mask of her own volition. She has been careful. They should go away, find someone else.

Every thump. Every bird cry. Every rattling of the water pipes makes her jump. She tells herself it's nothing. She is imagining danger. There was no man at the window—a trick of the light, the dark, the storm. But she keeps picturing them circling the cabin. She is afraid she has finally gone mad and will need to be returned to the hospital. Patty would come if Francine called. Her psychiatrist would send the police to help her. But she thinks she would sound crazy if she tried to explain what is happening. And she knows that in itself is crazy. She is caught in a loop of her own insanity.

The fear exhausts her, and she falls asleep.

When she wakes up, the cabin is dark and cold. She reaches for a flashlight. There is a black shape sitting at the end of couch. Francine inhales sharply but forgets to exhale. She squints, trying to rationalize what she is seeing. Her imagination has brought the threat inside with her. It's probably nothing more than bunched up blankets. But the figure moves.

"Hello, Francine."

Too paralyzed to react, she is easy prey.

He grabs her wrist and drags her from the sofa onto the floor. He straddles her, hard crotch grinding into her stomach. He pins her down, his knees on her arms.

Even though it is dark, shadows slide across his face, changing it from one thing to another. He produces a knife. "Hey, Francine, let's see if you're more than skin deep."

The cold tip of the blade at her hairline is like the pinprick of a needle. He starts at her forehead. The cutting feels like being burned—as if he has held the blade in fire.

Francine screams.

He works the blade down to her chin and then starts up the other side of her face. He stops cutting when the tip returns to the point where he started on her forehead. He then works the knife beneath the skin separating the top layer from the layer below. He peels it back starting from the top.

Francine continues to scream like the time in college. But this time it is real. He doesn't stop her. No one is around to hear her scream. No one comes out this far at night.

Delicately pinched between his thumbs and index fingers he holds up her skinned face for her to see. "Like a mask, don't you think?" He sets it aside and picks up the knife again. He puts the blade to her forehead once more. "Let's see how deep I can go."

Blood fills her mouth and nose. She spits and snorts, trying not to drown in her own fluids. She has been so wrong—all those years rejecting the idea that there was a repressed inner-self. All those years of her life lost to fear. They didn't turn a person into anything. They didn't need to. They came only to expose. Her fear of being turned into something else was unwarranted. Everyone had been right. It had always been inside her. Francine stops screaming.

As the man peels away the next layer, his eyes grow large at what he sees and his grin tightens into a thin line.

She knows what he has uncovered.

Beneath it all, the monstrous is finally revealed.

FARKELBERRY FORREST CEMETERY

By Tim Chizmar

In Farkelberry Forrest Cemetery, roughly six feet under the earth and dry rot, something unpleasant began to occur. A corpse, mostly rotted away and forgotten, lost to the ticking hands of time, began to stir. The corpse, still with pieces of a fine suit holding its innards together, opened its dead eyes, looked straight ahead and saw nothing but pure pitch-blackness everywhere. Fearing he was going blind, he began to panic before remembering where he was...

He grumbled; as memories of another life came flooding back. He tasted death all around. He was in a coffin, ironically, he had picked out himself. He'd always wondered what death tasted like and now he knew.

The taste of death reminded him of cinnamon mixed with vomit. Yes, definitely an unpleasant regurgitation of cinnamon flooded what was left of his throat. He coughed up bits of mold and dust.

His name had been Henry once. If his plans had been carried out properly, there was a tombstone somewhere high above that listed him as a devoted Father, Husband.

He was alive but also dead. This was some unfortunate news. While coming to life, his bony fingers reminded him of Rice Krispies as they snapped, crackled and popped. He reached out and scratched around.

Funny how people change from a person to just a body.
He touched the smoothness of the top of the casket. In

frustration, he kicked as hard as he could. Unfortunately, he just didn't have power in his weakened dilapidated state.

How long have I been under here?

Am I supposed to be alone in here forever?

I'll go crazy.

Henry heard a noise. He wasn't alone. There it was again. Something small was climbing up his pants. He twisted and kicked until his mysterious intruder settled on his chest. Something poked up between the buttons on his dress shirt. In the darkness, he could feel it looking at him. It was too small to be a rat, but much larger than a roach. Without much choice, Henry waited.

"Well Doodles, you gonna say hi?" a tiny voice said.

How could that be? He was alone. Surely he was mistaken, or perhaps he had gone completely insane?

"Relax Doodles, you is as sane as the day is long. Oh yeah, you's dead all right, Doodly, but I think you's all there and even if you was crazy like ol' B.G. Stickums in the plot behind yours, I'd still like you cause you're my *buddy*! I decided that I'm not gonna leave your side all night long."

All night? Henry thought. *What's so special about this night? What's going on?*

"Doodles, c'mon its Halloweener you silly stooopids! It's time for the Dad to walk the earth, and with you beings all locked in here I thought I'd say hi."

It's not time for the Dad *to walk the earth...*

"Did you have kids?"

Yes.

"Did you kick the bucket?"

Apparently.

"Then looks like the Dad shall walk the Earth! I'm a pretty smart worm!"

Henry tried to scream with all his might, yet, when he tried, his jaw fell to the side with a creak and a thud. He tried to hold on to whatever reason he had left.

You are not a worm because worms do not talk.

"Golly mister, you sure are smart! Say...you learn in people school that dead bodies wake up on Halloweener, or is that like the worms-not-talking thing?"

I'd rather not hear from you. Leave me be.

"All alone to rot by yourself? Not a chance, Doodles. I brought you the gift of stories!"

Henry felt the presence of a book being pulled on his belly.

Stories? Are they good?

Henry remembered reading his favorite stories to his children as they were growing up.

"They're the best! and they's all written by the Horror Writer's Association, so you know they's good stuff."

Henry gave in to the moment and his predicament and to this charming little creature.

That sounds good he thought, *as long as I'm in here I might as well be entertained by a cute little whimsical, talking worm. My grandkids would probably find you cute.*

"Oh I don't know about that, Doodles. Remember when I said I was a talking worm?"

Yes.

"I lied"

Oh.

"I'm a tapeworm, and I'm here because your organs are now working again. As I'm reading you these stories I'm going to be feeding off your meat, Doodles. You taste *so* good."

No.

As the pages of the book opened and the worm read passages out loud, Henry felt the full length of this flatworm burrowing deep in his split stomach lining.

They say that to this day on Halloween, visitors standing over the grave of Henry Doodle can still hear the reading of macabre holiday-inspired tales mixed with a sucking sound and a very weak attempt to scream...

HALLOWEEN IN EAST HAMPTON

Robin Wyatt Dunn

That Halloween, the children of East Hampton appreciated my costume and we got to talking as I stood at the
door with my candy bag. I had taken up trick-or-treating
since my daughter died to honor her memory, and so I
stood there that late evening in October in my best bear
costume, brown and fuzzy, with plastic whiskers clipped
to my nose and rubber ears attached to the top of my head.

"Come inside, sir," said the little girl, who looked disturbingly like my daughter, dressed in some kind of light
blue fairy outfit. Next to her was a small, red ladybird, a
round fat child of indeterminate age, and a little wizard-boy, perhaps six.

"You all look so nice," I said.

"So do you," said the little fairy, and beckoned me in.

Inside the home was very 70s, with a brown shag carpet,
and orange wallpaper. I could smell coffee and incense.

"Your candy," said the ladybird, the little red one, I think
he was a boy. He dropped some packaged candies into my
plastic supermarket bag. I barely noticed. I was convinced,
suddenly, that my daughter was in the house. She hadn't
died in the car accident after all! I could almost smell her
perfume, the kind she would wear when she dressed up as
Janice Joplin.

"You should eat some of the candy, sir," said the blue
fairy, her eyes strangely affecting.

"It smells like you have coffee!" I said.

"Get him some coffee," said the blue fairy to the wizard-boy, who stomped off to the linoleum-floored kitchen, displeased with his chore.

It smelled delicious, that coffee.

I noticed the little girl was unwrapping one of the peanut butter candies and shoving it into my mouth, standing on her tip toes.

"Chew it up," she said.

I did, as I walked into the kitchen, following the coffee aroma.

The small wizard-boy pushed down the French press, with special care, his brow furrowed with concentration. His skin was very pale.

"Thank you, son," I said. "Aren't you a handsome wizard!"

"I'm a warlock," he said. "Like Charlie Sheen."

I laughed. "You certainly are! You certainly are. Thank you for the coffee. Say, do you kids know my daughter, Stephanie?"

The wizard-boy finished pouring the coffee and the little ladybird (I think he was a boy) poured some cream into the cup, which was very nice of him and presented me with the steaming mug.

"Your parents sure taught you nice manners!" I exclaimed. I took a sip; it was delicious, hot coffee.

"He's drinking it," said the ladybird.

"Your daughter is this way," said the blue fairy.

I dropped the coffee mug on the floor and followed her down the hall, feeling right, for the first time since my daughter died, two years before.

The hallway was filled with smoke and incense, and the little blue fairy held my hand.

"You're going to feel a little strange," she said. "But you'll get used to it. Now, take a deep breath!"

I did as she said, and she swung open the door to one of the bedrooms, also appointed in an affected 70s style, with avocado-colored cushions and reddish browns sucking up all the available light. What light there was, hovered over the face of the man in the room, who wore bright white make-up, somewhat like a clown. He had wide eyes and a terrible smile or rictus on his face. Several lamps pointed up at him.

"Say hello to the Clown Man," said the little blue fairy, quickly departing the room and shutting the door behind her.

I chewed the remainder of the peanut candy that had stuck to my teeth, staring at the man.

"What a house you have here!" I said. "A real scary factory! I mean, a fine haunted house!"

"I'm glad you like it," the Clown said. "It's wonderful to be here." His voice was surprisingly deep.

"Say . . . that little girl, she said my daughter was here! Do you know where she is?"

"Yes," said the Clown. "I do."

I found myself on my knees.

"Please. Where? Show me, will you?"

The Clown, who had been standing straight, his back right against the wall as he regarded me with his huge eyes, now took a step toward me and lay his hand on my head. It was comfortable and warm.

"Such a poor man you are," he said. "So unhappy. Would you like to make these poor children happy?"

"Yes. Yes I would," I said. I stared at the wall, smelling the incense.

"They will be very grateful," said the Clown.

"Yes," I said. "I understand."

"Good!" said the Clown cheerily. "Now stand up!"

I did as he instructed, chewing the last scrap of peanut-sugar from my rear tooth.

"Let's get you out of this bear shirt," said the Clown-man. "There's an outfit we'll need you to wear."

"All right." I left on my furry pants but obliged the man and removed my shirt. To my surprise, he removed a can of makeup from his pocket and immediately smeared it across my chest. It was very cool and felt good.

"There we are," he said. "Let's get you all covered up." He covered my torso in white, asking me to turn to so he could cover every inch of my skin.

"Now you do your face," he said, handing me the jar, and unclipping the bear whiskers from my nose.

I stared into the Clown's eyes as I applied the makeup. At length he nodded.

"How do you feel?" the Clown man asked.

"A little dizzy," I confessed.

"Water!" shouted the clown, and the little blue fairy girl came back in, holding a cool glass to my lips. I sipped it gratefully.

"Are you ready?" asked the Clown man.

"Yes," I said, taking a deep breath.

The little blue fairy girl looked at me with admiration as the Clown led me back out of the room. The wizard-boy and the ladybird ran up to whisper something to the fairy-girl but she shushed them and they continued to watch, as the Clown held my hand and led me further down the hallway.

"You'll do fine," said the Clown. "Just remember, be yourself, and no hard feelings."

With that he was gone, and I was alone in the smoke, walking ahead, the paint sticky on my skin. I wished I'd had more of the candy, or a hat filled with coffee, like a beer-nozzle hat I could wear on my head, but for coffee, just for a situation like this one, but it was too late now. I was committed, and the smoke smelled delicious, some-how familiar. I stepped up onto the stage at the end of the hall; the altar.

There were a great many blinking lights glued to the altar; they reminded me of the kind man at the welfare office who always had many blinking and shiny objects at his window to relieve some of the crushing depression of that place.

The level of smoke was increasing, and, in truth, I did find it a little difficult to breathe. Though I had quit smoking the year previous, my lungs were still weak. Then I heard the children and the Clown Man crying at me from just out of sight behind the smoke:

"Look down, under the rabbit, you'll find the knife!"

I looked down. Sure enough, a white plush bunny with huge, soulful eyes regarded me. A red ribbon had been tied around its neck. I moved it aside with my toe and saw the metal beneath.

"Now the bowl!" said the fairy-girl. I recognized her voice.

For a moment, I remembered my daughter again, and I turned my head, squinting through the smoke.

The fairy-girl spoke again, "Go ahead!" She was excited.

Cheap photos of Elvis ripped from magazines and others of svelte fashion models, male and female, alternated with National-Geographic-style pictures of woodland animals covered the altar. Foxes, marmots, antelope. In one, a huge bear gazed into my eyes and I was able to relax a bit.

The bowl was at the foot of the altar, nestled within several antelope horns.

For some reason I couldn't explain, I understood what I had to do.

I picked up the knife and dug the point of it into my wrist, pressing in until a small trickle of blood oozed out. I squeezed my skin, to allow the blood to drip into the bowl.

"Yes!" shouted the Clown.

"Give him another piece of candy," I heard the little

ladybird-boy say, and I was grateful to feel the fairy girl fingers against my lips, offering another peanut-sweet. I chewed it gratefully as the Clown-man pressed me gently back against the prickly antelope horns at the back of the altar.

"My daughter!" I said.

"She's here in our hearts," said the Clown-man.

The wizard-boy laughed.

"As you will be, John."

I felt very right. Things weren't perfect, but they were close. Somehow I had found the people I needed.

HOLLYWOOD ENDING

By R. B. Payne

Dia de los Muerte

Sunset Strip, 2 a.m.

A half-naked girl dances,
a drink slops in her hand.

Sweating. Pulsating.

She wants fame.
That's the movie business.
It's easy enough to take her home.

Tonight I am Brad Pitt's eyes,
George Clooney's chin,
and a dash of Errol Flynn.

I lure the weak ones.

The Mariachi band sings:

Al vivo todo le falta y al muerto todo le sobra.

The ones alive need everything, the dead need nothing.

Laurel Canyon, outside.

A pack of coyotes how.
A rabbit gives its life for the greater good.

Inside.

"Hey," she says, slipping out of her bra and panties.
"Why aren't you getting undressed?"
She anticipates my kiss.

I crystallize.
Fingers sharp as knives and cold as arctic wind
slip into her belly.

She hisses.
My icy touch, her dark sweet mass.
She stiffens.

I raise her body to my shoulder
and unlock the door to the cellar.

The family waits.

We always eat in the cold room.

JOHNNY JACKSON'S SCHOOL DARE

By P.S. Gifford

Johnny Jackson scowled as he jaunted arrogantly into the lunch room. Please understand he always scowled; he was just that sort of a 14-year-old. His short, cropped red hair was spiked, as always, and large silver braces adorned his front teeth—adding further to his menacing appearance. Johnny, or J.J. as he was appropriately nicknamed, had always been a particularly large kid, and these days he was at least a foot taller than most of the other kids in school—and even taller than a lot of the teachers, for that matter!

Philip Michaels and Keith Leicester winced, glancing at each other uncomfortably as J.J. spotted them and then quickly marched purposefully in their direction. As today's target was now obvious, the other pupils sighed in relief. They knew that they were safe, at least for that day. Philip and Keith tried to prepare themselves as they watched J.J., dressed in his usual camouflage pants, green T-shirt and laced up black boots, menacingly approach them.

J.J. stared at the two trembling boys for what seemed like an hour, but it was only really about 24 and a half seconds. He grinned with satisfaction and rubbed his grubby hands together as he watched his victims wiggle and squirm in fear.

J.J. put his hands emphatically on his hips and looked around to see if any teachers were watching. Seeing that the coast was clear, he turned back to the squirming pair.

"So, worms!" he finally muttered. "Do you have the five pounds protection money for me?"

Without hesitation, Keith and Philip reached frantically into their pockets and rustled about. Keith was soon triumphant; he still had his week's pocket money intact and hurriedly placed it on the table. Johnny scooped it up hastily and stuffed it into the back pocket of his dirty trousers.

J.J. then focused on Philip, who had assembled a pile of coins on the table. He prayed as he counted it out that it would be enough.

Panic filled his eyes as he counted. Why, oh, why did I buy that bag of chips last night at the fish and chip shop? he moaned to himself.

The whole lunch room was silent now, watching the horrible scene unfold, yet too scared to help. Four pounds and twenty-seven pence lay on the table. J.J. stared at Philip; Philip stared back at J.J., terrified.

"I s'pose it is gonna have to do then," J.J. scoffed sarcastically. "But this is because you are short."

As he spoke he picked up the carton of chocolate low-fat milk Philip had been enjoying with his cheese and onion sandwich. Leisurely, and with a lot of hand waving and dramatic flair to make sure that every kid in the room was paying full attention, he poured it very slowly over Philip's head.

Howls of laughter filled the lunch room while tears filled Philip's eyes. J.J., looking smug and triumphant, placed the rest of the money in his trouser pocket, and picking up the other half of the cheese and onion sandwich, he swaggered out of the lunch room.

~

That night Keith and Philip did their homework together at Philip's house as they munched on delicious sausage rolls and mugs of tea. Philip was still frustrated and angry at the afternoon's humiliating incident.

"He can't keep treating people like that!" he grumbled as he took another sip of his tea. "Someone is going to have to teach that big, ugly twit a lesson."

Suddenly Philip felt strangely inspired. "Wait! I have got a great idea!" he announced excitedly." Why don't we play a trick on him?" he continued, surprised by the sudden thrill the notion of revenge had given him.

Keith was intrigued, but raised a doubting eyebrow as he studied the look now on his best friend's freckled face. "Go on," he prompted. "I'm listening."

"You know the old spooky overgrown graveyard just a short way from Whitely Common? They haven't used it in years. Why don't we make a bet with Johnny in front of the whole lunch room that he is too chicken to go there at midnight and collect an envelope we are going to plant there?"

Keith thoughtfully nodded. "But that's too easy! I reckon that J.J. isn't afraid of much, and he will be able to do that real easy."

"Ah, yes. But here's the thing. I want you to secretly borrow your dad's camcorder, and I am going to play dress up! Last Halloween, if you recall, my mum dressed me up as a really menacing ghoul. Don't you remember? When I came knocking on your door to go trick and treating, you didn't even recognize me! What I plan to do is wear the costume and hide myself in the graveyard, and just as Johnny goes to reach for the envelope, I will jump out and make lots of moaning and groaning sounds and scare the life out of him! And you will be there filming it all on the old camcorder! Then we can send it to him, and tell him what we did, and let him know that if he continues bullying us or anyone else, we will show it to everyone in school!"

And as the two of them chatted further as they finished their supper and homework they got more and more excited!

~

It was three days later when the plan began to fall into place, on a fateful, nippy and rainy November afternoon. Once more Keith and Philip were sitting in the lunch room minding their own business, and once more Johnny had marched in scowling. For the last few days he had picked on other victims, but today was once more going to be their turn again.

As J.J. marched over, the two boys prayed silently and stood up to face him. J.J. was obviously a little taken aback. His victims usually cowered and got all wobbly kneed at his mere presence.

"Do you have my protection money?" he demanded.

Philip and Keith just stood there.

"Well?" Johnny yelled.

"I bet you think you are afraid of no one or nothing:" Keith bravely replied. "Being the great protector and all."

Johnny was both amazed and shocked. No one had ever stood up to him before. He also was extremely aware that all the kids in the lunch room were now holding their breath, waiting to see what was going to happen next.

"How about you prove just how brave you are?" Philip added, surprised he was even able to speak with his mouth being as dry as the Sahara desert.

J.J. squinted at him. He was surely going to have to think very quickly if he was to maintain his reign of terror. And thinking isn't what he did best. He considered the possibility of simply thumping them, but he realized that would make him look as if he was afraid, in front of all these other kids, at whatever plan they had in mind. No, he had no choice. He was going to have to go along with it.

"You betcha' I ain't afraid of nuttin' or nobody," he said

finally, biting his lower lip.

The two friends breathed a sigh of relief in unison, and as the entire lunchroom listened on intently, Keith continued.

"Okay, here is the dare we have in mind. On this Saturday night, just before midnight we will leave our ten pounds protection money in a brown envelope and attach it to the old crypt—you know the one I mean. Everyone does; it is the one that is right dead center in the graveyard! All you have to do is simply go and get it and bring it to school on Monday morning. If you are successful, you will have proven to everyone just how brave and tough you truly are. But we'll be back in the graveyard at 1:00 a.m. to check, and if you have failed to retrieve it, then we shall take it and bring it to school instead."

Johnny listened to the proposition He hated that old, spooky, graveyard. At the best of times it gave him the creeps, and they wanted him to go at midnight? Still, he did have a reputation to uphold. He glared at all the curious, expectant eyes in the lunchroom carefully scrutinizing him.

"Deal!" he finally said as he contorted his face into the biggest scowl imaginable. Next he promptly turned about, and stormed out of the lunch room stamping his boots on the floor and muttering angrily under his breath as he went.

Keith and Philip could scarcely believe their luck at getting away with it and could not wait till Saturday night!

~

Saturday finally came, and the two boys text-messaged each other, deciding the final details. Both of the friends had to begrudgingly spend the day with their parents, shopping and doing chores, but at eleven thirty they promised each other to sneak out of the house, ride their bikes to the graveyard, and take their respective places.

Keith couldn't sleep that night. He just lay there watching the clock methodically ticking away. When at long last it reached eleven, he quietly got up and put on his black sweatshirt and dark blue jeans. Nervously he made his way down the staircase, taking particular care not to tread on the steps he knew always creaked. His parents, although in bed, were notoriously light sleepers, and if they awoke his plans would be ruined. Finally he quietly made it to the bottom and stealthily entered his father's study where the new digital camcorder was kept. His father would be furious if he knew Keith had borrowed it. Yet the rewards of embarrassing J.J. once and for all made it a justifiable risk. He put on his anorak and quietly sneaked out the back kitchen door.

Ten minutes later he was pedaling furiously towards the graveyard. The damp, cold November sky allowed almost no moonlight, and a soft hazy fog was forming, rising from the ground. This is going to be perfect, he thought to himself. Absolutely perfect!

He arrived at the graveyard at 11:45 p.m., which left plenty of time. He saw no sign of Philip and figured he must have arrived earlier and was already in place behind the crypt, as he was always so reliable. Keith chained his bike on the fence far away from the entrance, hoping J.J. wouldn't see it. With his heart beating furiously, he swung open the graveyard gate; it seemed to complain and whine with an unearthly screech. He was startled by the horrible sound for a moment, which seemed to echo all about him. He took a deep breath of the cold night air in an attempt to steady his jumpy nerves and cautiously he entered the cemetery grounds.

Keith approached the crypt, which, in the dark misty shadows looked larger and creepier at night and appeared a hundred times more terrifying than he remembered. He pulled out a large brown envelope with the initials "J.J." boldly written in blood-colored ink and with trembling fingers attached it to the gate. Once more, he glanced at his watch. Seven minutes till midnight. Perfect. He headed towards an old, crumbling, long-since-forgotten tombstone just a few feet from the crypt—the ideal place to hide. He positioned himself on the soggy cold grass, pulled out the camcorder, and sat there waiting.

He did not have long to wait at all, dear reader, for just a scant few minutes later he heard the telltale sign that someone else had arrived; the eerie screeching of the old gate at the entrance. He hoped that Philip was ready!

As he peered into the darkness, Keith detected a large figure slowly approaching. As the figure gradually got closer and closer he saw it was indeed J.J.! The game was afoot! Yet he looked different to Keith. His arrogant expression had been replaced by another look, a look that Keith recognized all too well—fear.

J.J. was now only a few feet from Keith's safe hiding place, just in front of the crypt, and Keith held his breath as he saw him look about suspiciously. After what seemed to Keith like a year, J.J. took one step towards it and then paused, almost as if he was changing his mind. But then, he took another step closer, and another, and another. Keith filmed as he saw J.J.'s shaking hand reach out to grab the envelope. But then, just as his stubby fingers were about to grasp it, suddenly from the darkness a figure sprang up!

J.J. instantly recoiled. He stepped backwards. His eyes were wide and his face terrified. Then it happened—the unimaginable—he screamed! Not just any old scream, let me tell you dear reader. Oh no, this was a scream to waken the very dead themselves!

Keith could not believe his luck as he filmed the scene unfolding before him. Philip's costume and makeup was even better than he had remembered. His face looked as if it was half-rotted away and one eye dangled precariously out of its socket. And as a long, bony finger pointed in J.J.'s direction, J.J. gave out another scream, perhaps even louder than the first, and it echoed into the shadowy night. He turned around and scurried back to the entrance. As a jubilant Keith continued to film, J.J. slipped on the damp grass, flailing his arms and legs in the air like a rag doll. Then he fumbled awkwardly back to his feet and continued on his way back to the entrance, never once looking behind him.

Keith victoriously chased after him and continued to film as J.J. jumped onto his bike, and rode off frantically!

A very satisfied Keith made his way back over to the crypt, retrieved the envelope and stuffed it into his jeans pocket. He looked about for Philip.

"Hey, where are you hiding Philip? That was great," he cried. "Anyway, I have got to get home before my parents realize I am gone. I will see you tomorrow and we can have a right old giggle about it!"

Moments later Keith was once more on his bike, grinning from ear to ear as he peddled along on the late night bike ride home.

~

The next morning, whilst lying in bed, his mum knocked on his bedroom door.

"Wake up sleepy bones! Philip's on the phone for you!" Yawning and still half asleep, Keith clambered downstairs to the phone.

"Hello, Philip! Wasn't last night absolutely brilliant! I have to admit, your costume was so bloomin' good, it almost scared me!"

There was silence from the other end of the phone.

"Philip, are you there, mate?"

"Uh, um, uh, yes I am here...but I don't understand. I was just calling to apologize!" Philip stammered. "My parents caught me just as I was trying to sneak out of the house last night; I got into loads of bother with them, let me tell you. I wanted to say how sorry I am for not showing up."

THE OLD MAGIC

By Xach Fromson

The motion sensitive witch decoration cackled when Gretchen passed in front of it.

"Oh, shut up," she said, fixing it with a glare. The witch deactivated, its glowing red eyes winking out.

Gretchen hardly had room to stand inside the frozen yogurt store. It was full of people in various costumes trying to beat the unusually warm Halloween heat. Gretchen wouldn't have even been there herself if it wasn't eighty-seven degrees at sunset. The crowds were coming out to play, which suited her needs just fine. But a crowd like this was a little unreasonable. The majority of the women in the store and on the patio were wearing their Leg Avenue uniforms. Sexy bee. Sexy nurse. Sexy cop. Sexy turtle. Sexy ninja. Sexy Disney princess. Some women pranced around actually trying to be sexy horses. And buzzing around them, like vultures with peacock aesthetics, were the *dudebros*. The buzz-cut-sporting, barbed-wire-tattooed cavemen wore togas with neckties, Viking helmets, or any of a litany of tired tropes that had remained disturbingly constant since the 1980s.

Somewhere, Gretchen thought, civilization had taken a hard left turn and veered straight for insanity.

The crowd was young, mid-twenties to mid-thirties she guessed, but none of them were particularly exciting. Sure, a few of the costumes were impressive, but that wasn't what she was looking for. Not tonight.

Gretchen was just about to give up on this crowd and venture back out, when she heard it. The soft giggle coming from near the cash register was like a rain stick, like glass shards tinkling in a trash bin. It was musical without any score behind the notes, and it was full of life. It was exactly the sound Gretchen had been hoping to hear.

When she saw the woman belonging to the wonderful laugh, Gretchen only felt more vindicated in trusting her instincts. The woman was petite, blonde and perky in all the obnoxious ways that so many young women tried to replicate these days. She was dressed as some kind of fairy pixie-type creature, with small wings strapped to her back. When she moved, the light reflected off hundreds of tiny flecks of pink glitter that the girl had smeared over herself, doubtless because it made her feel like a real fairy.

The glitter pixie had her arm around the elbow of a dudebro who was paying for one big cup of frozen yogurt and two spoons. He was dressed as some kind of a generic vampire with slicked back hair and a cape. When he turned to the pixie girl, Gretchen saw that his face was painted white and he had fake fangs.

"Baby, I told you," he said, "it's fat free."

"Would you like a lid for that?" The woman at the cash register looked bored to death but was putting on a brave face. She gave the dudebro vampire a fake smile.

"Nah, we'll just eat it on the patio," he said. He handed a credit card to the cashier, and leaned in to kiss his arm candy. She turned her cheek to him.

"Hey, how come you're not dressed up?" The pixie girl's voice was not what Gretchen was expecting. It wasn't high pitched or squeaky. If anything, it was a good deal lower than a squeak. She had the voice of a grown woman, full of energy, full of life.

"Manager said we have to wear the uniform," the cashier shrugged.

"Well, I hope you have fun anyway!"

The couple whispered right past her and out onto the patio. The energy coming off of them was palpable. They smelled of roses after a rain, of lightning storms, of freshly turned dirt. And they were completely oblivious of her.

Absentmindedly, Gretchen moved her way through the line and got her own small bowl of frozen yogurt. The couple out on the patio was humming, sending off thrums of life that pulsed through the air, pulsed through her skin, made her own heart beat with their rhythm. She didn't even realize she'd gotten peanut butter yogurt until she took her first bite of it.

The thrumming was strongest on this night. Gretchen could always feel the energy from people around her, but as Samhain approached, her sensitivities intensified. Until tonight, when they reached a climax. Every person was an instrument, playing a part in the great orchestra of the crowd, and she was the only audience member who could feel all the notes. Their vitality thrilled her, sending chills up her arms.

She found a table on the patio with only one chair. Gretchen took the seat.

The couple laughed. Hers was a melody that seemed to ripple underneath his, bringing out lower notes in his laughter, giving it a richness that made it sensual. He threw his head back and laughed from deep in his belly, a hearty sound that sent all the hairs on Gretchen's neck upright with desire.

She leaned on the table, the yogurt forgotten and melting. Dozens of people walked past them, going to or from bars and restaurants, going to parties or back home. Some had kids with plastic pails of candy. The vampire and his glitter pixie watched them go by. He called out to several of them, complimenting them on their costumes. Gretchen noticed none of them. She was deep in the throes of the old magic now.

Gretchen had grown careful, rarely venturing where people would spot her, catching a passerby only every few years on Samhain. She got to know every age spot that showed on her pale skin, every yellowed fingernail, every wrinkle. Several times years would go by, and she'd have nothing to do but watch herself age, the outskirts of towns and villages being her only contact with the world. But time moved on, and people's fears faded, replaced by new ones. Diseases, wars, religions, progress. The world changed; it expanded. Instead of villages and towns looking within for a reason to fear, they began to look outward. They hated the others, but protected themselves and each other. Gretchen had slowly grown accustomed to people, as living far from cities became impractical. She had adapted again, learning to stay invisible in the crowds, learning to stay in sight but out of mind.

Every Halloween, people went missing or ran away. There were so many of them now, no one thought much of the occasional disappearance. People moved on. They never looked twice. And the less attention they paid to each other, the easier it became for her to take one every year.

Gretchen's age spots hadn't bothered her for decades now. Her skin, pale and smooth showed no hints of a wrinkle; her fingernails were clear and unbroken, the yellow long forgotten. And with the old magic lost to the others so long ago, Gretchen knew no one could stop her ever again.

The glitter pixie moved to leave, pulling the vampire up with her. Even if Gretchen hadn't seen the shimmering air thrum more intensely around the woman, she would still have known what was going on. Magic was hardly necessary to see what was plainly evident on the woman's face. She leaned in and whispered something to the vampire, and the two of them hopped over the ropes separating the patio from the sidewalk.

Gretchen slipped through the crowd to follow them,

careful to keep enough distance from her prey without losing them into the night.

This was the part where she felt more alive than any other night of the year. The end was coming closer moment by moment, and all the reasons Gretchen had to hide herself and her abilities every other night were slipping away. She reached out with her energy and pulled the shadows in around her. The darkness wrapped her in its warmth; it comforted her and supported her. The darkness whispered in her ear, chanting things that she first heard so long ago. The world dimmed as she faded out of it. People passed by her without ever knowing she was next to them, oblivious to how close they came to touching death. But the two shapes up ahead stayed bright, beacons of energy and vitality that Gretchen was about to make her own. Gretchen's stomach fluttered in anticipation. It was a meal like no other. The coppery flavor of blood was so close that she could taste it. The sweetness, the warmth as it filled her body with their lives, was indescribable. Her skin, when she thought about it, tightened up. Her body yearned for it so badly that she felt the beginnings of it already. She had to strike soon, or she would risk losing her focus and getting swept up in the sensation.

The glitter pixie turned onto a residential side street, pulling the vampire with her. They left the bright streetlights behind, weak bulbs that only dimly lit the houses offering them, and Gretchen, more privacy. No people were on this street. The children had trick-or-treated themselves home. No Jack-O-Lanterns lit porches or patios. Everyone was far from home or safe in bed.

Gretchen flung her energy outward. It seeped into the street, crawled up the light posts, oozed over the cars parked along the curb. It tugged at the darkness, pulling it closer, making it denser. The shadows grew thicker ahead of her, congealing around the pixie girl and her vampire.

They were drunk on each other, so focused on what lay ahead of them that neither one saw the thickening dark.

In the old days, people would drive their cattle between bonfires to protect them. It was a meaningless gesture, since Gretchen never once went after cattle, but she liked the look of it all the same. She searched with her energy, feeling for light posts with frayed wires, while she walked in the middle of the street. She was far enough behind them that they wouldn't see her if they turned around. They'd see shadows, maybe, but not her. They wouldn't see her in the darkness, staring at them with a predator's eyes.

Two light posts, directly across from each other, sparked when her energy washed over the wires, jolting her with a touch of their electricity. The lights flickered, a fitting creepy moment for Halloween.

The glitter pixie stopped to look at them, and she jumped when they flickered again. The vampire wrapped his arms around her.

Gretchen couldn't hear what they were saying, but it didn't matter now.

The glitter pixie leaned into the vampire, rising up on her toes to kiss him. She pushed him gently back, keeping only a sliver of light between their lips, until the vampire's back rested against the streetlight. She flicked her tongue out, licking the vampire's fake fangs. Gretchen pushed her energy into the light posts, surging the power.

The bulbs grew brighter, humming against the darkness that Gretchen had brought to press against them all. The hum turned into a whine, and the bulbs simultaneously exploded, shattering the glass tops to the light posts in a pair of brilliant flashes.

Gretchen twisted her energy in the wires, infusing her magic with her will, and jets of flame erupted from the two shattered posts. The flames flared up and created exactly the spectacle that Gretchen wanted. This was the moment she dreamed of all year long. These two poor fools couldn't possibly comprehend what was about to happen. They had no way to stop it, no way to protect or defend themselves. Oh, if they'd remembered the old magic, they could have stood a chance. But they were just rats, and she had sprung her trap on them.

She pulled back on the flames, bringing them lower and dimmer, like old gas lamps. There was no longer any need for her to hide in the shadows, and she stepped out of her cloak of darkness, toward them. She stood in the middle of the street, her pale skin shining with her own power.

Finally, the vampire and the pixie girl saw her. They hadn't seen her at the yogurt store. They hadn't seen her following them, but they were seeing her now.

She made herself a spectacle to behold, drawing up to her full height and holding her arms out at her sides.

Oh, what they must be thinking. How terrified they must be as they frantically tried to figure out what was happening, and why. She wouldn't explain it to them. Why would she explain to her prey that she was their only natural predator? What a waste of time. They would die with the question on their tongues. They didn't deserve to know the answer. Food doesn't get to ask why.

She summoned her energy, focusing it into her hands. The weight of it increased until she held two orbs of pure magic ready to unleash on whatever she commanded it to. She hurled them. She felt the orbs hit, felt the glitter pixie and the vampire come under her control.

They tried to move. Their eyes widened as they struggled against her. But she had honed her willpower over centuries of constant use, strengthening it every time. There was nothing they could do now, no way for them to escape. No help was coming.

The electricity would do nicely. It lacked the flourish of real lightning, but with no clouds in the sky, Gretchen didn't want to spend the extra energy creating a storm just for these two. They didn't deserve the show. She needed to taste their life, feel it replenish and renew her. She wasn't about to deny herself that satisfaction. She reached out for the light posts again, turning her energy inside them and calling forth the crackling white arcs that flowed underneath the streets.

She was about to pull it through them both when she made an impulsive decision. She wanted to stretch this moment out, feel it wash over her in wave after wave of ecstasy. The girl would watch helplessly as Gretchen took the vampire's life into herself. She would see that all her beauty and all her youth couldn't save her in the face of true power. And Gretchen would take the moment, savor it, let it roll across her tongue. She would take all the pleasure from the vampire and ride the feeling until it just started to fade. Right then, right before she felt the first pulls of time on her body, she would take the girl. This glitter pixie was going to watch her world get destroyed, and Gretchen was going to break her pathetic mind before she consumed her.

Gretchen held the glitter pixie in place with one hand, held her still, forced her to watch. With the other she called forth the electricity from the light pole. It jolted out just the way a lightning bolt would. The flash of light connected the vampire's suspended body to the streetlight. His body shuddered and spasmed as the electricity danced over his skin.

Gretchen felt electricity penetrating his body, pouring through every inch of him. She felt him try to scream but denied it to him. Then she called the electricity into her. It cut through the air, creating a jagged arc between the palm of her outstretched hand and the vampire's body. When it hit her, she felt herself light up from within. His energy was so young, so full of life and potential. She felt it lift her off the ground, her hair floating away from her shoulders. The boy had so much in him, Gretchen felt like she was going to burst from drawing it all in at once.

And then it was over. The light winked out, Gretchen's feet were back on the asphalt, and where there had been two there was now only the glitter pixie and a lingering smell of ozone.

The girl's eyes had widened to great big orbs. They looked like bug eyes, ready to fall out of her head. But Gretchen didn't feel her trying to scream, or even trying to struggle and break free of her energy. This wasn't what she wanted. She wanted the girl to fight, to resist. She wanted to see the girl refuse to accept what was about to happen. She wanted to sweeten the girl's energy by knowing that she had first crushed her spirit. But she simply hung there, waiting for the end. And Gretchen decided not to make her wait long for it. She called the electricity forth from the other streetlight, and watched as it zapped the glitter pixie. She felt the lightning pulse through the pixie's body. She reached out her hand to pull the girl's life energy into herself. The girl was full of even more than her vampire companion had been. So much energy. More than Gretchen had ever found in a single person before. This was going to be amazing.

"Enough!" The glitter pixie screamed the word at Gretchen.

Gretchen recoiled.

The girl was still under Gretchen's control. How was she speaking? What was going on? Gretchen redoubled her will, focusing solely on restraining the girl while the electricity surged through her body.

The girl pulled her arms down to her sides. Her feet touched the asphalt, and she stood facing Gretchen with electricity dancing over her.

How was this happening? Gretchen looked around at

the street. The shadows were still in place. The streetlights had exploded. The entire block was quiet. She hadn't done anything wrong. So how was this girl standing against her? She couldn't have a ward. Nobody knew how to make them anymore. The old magic was gone.

Gretchen pulled at the shadows to hide herself. She wasn't going to let this girl go, but she needed to change her attack. She felt the shadows begin to swirl toward her, but they stopped just out of her reach.

"Who the hell do you think you are?" the glitter pixie demanded.

Gretchen didn't have time to wonder how the girl was doing this. A wall of magical energy knocked her back several steps. It broke her concentration, and the shadows snapped back into place. The world brightened, the flames in the streetlights sputtered and went out. Behind her, Gretchen could hear music from the street. She heard people laugh. She heard cars drive by. Gretchen felt the girl's magic push against her, through her. It probed her mind, pulling at strands of thoughts and memories, holding her still while it searched through everything about her.

"Gretchen Hillyard," the girl said. She walked toward Gretchen. A faint glow emanated from the girl's skin.

"How do you know my name?" she asked.

"That is your name now, but it wasn't always," the girl said. "You haven't gone by your true name in a long time."

Gretchen tried to shield herself from the girl's magic, but no matter how strong she made her protections, it didn't seem to help.

The girl didn't seem to notice. She continued talking in the same smooth voice.

"It's a shame, really. If you had been paying attention, you would have seen that our names are no longer something to hide from. Our names no longer mark us." She twirled in the middle of the road, arms raised high.

"They've forgotten about us, Gretchen Hillyard," she

said loudly. "They've forgotten that names hold power."

"Who are you?" Gretchen asked. Her voice was trembling. Her voice hadn't trembled in centuries. More than centuries. She was feeling things that she hadn't felt in so long, she had almost forgotten their names.

Gretchen was afraid. She was scared and she didn't know what to do.

The girl smiled at her, and it was a predator's smile.

"My name," the girl said, "is Amena."

Gretchen's mind went flying down long forgotten memories, trying to find the name anywhere in her past. She couldn't remember ever meeting anyone named Amena. Was it possible she'd forgotten?

"We've never met before," Amena said to her. "I was old long before you were ever born."

Gretchen's mind frantically searched. "Oh, god," she whispered. The name Amena had been used in incantations she'd been taught as a girl. The name was as old as the old magic.

"I'm sorry," Gretchen said. "I didn't know."

"That doesn't matter." Amena closed the gap between the two of them. She reached out for Gretchen.

Gretchen tried to move away, but her body wouldn't follow her mind's orders. She was struck, and the witch was coming for her.

"But—"

"You took what was mine," Amena placed her hand over Gretchen's mouth. "Now I'm taking it back."

Amena's power seared through Gretchen. It burned through her mind and scorched her body, tearing away every piece of energy that bound her together. Gretchen tried to summon up her own magic to push away, but anything she called up was immediately ripped out of her. She felt it flow into Amena's hands, felt herself becoming a part of Amena.

Years of memories passed through her thoughts, flowing into the ancient woman. She was staring up at the stars. There were stone buildings, thatched roofs burning. Waves breaking on rocky shores. There was water washing over her bare feet. She saw a boy with a mane of red hair and blue eyes. He was leaning in to kiss her. Stone buildings covered in moss, no roofs on any of them. The road was cobblestone. Waves breaking against rocky shores. Ruins, only a few stones where buildings once stood. A paved road with electric streetlights. Now cities. Tall buildings everywhere. Lights everywhere. So many skylines. Views from houses on hills and from apartments. From cities and suburbs. And faces. So many faces. Every color, every type of face. Some were bony, some were round. Boys' faces. Girls' faces. All of them young. All of them blank. They didn't understand. They didn't know.

She felt herself losing her power, losing herself. She had the lives of so many of her victims inside her, so many lifetimes of energy, that what took only moments with the vampire stretched out beyond anything that Gretchen could comprehend. Her sense of time was gone, eclipsed by the pain. Moments of her life, moments of the lives she'd claimed, were being ripped out of her in a never-ending stream of agony. She tried to scream, but Amena held her hand firmly against Gretchen's mouth, and her willpower overwhelmed Gretchen so completely that even the desire to scream was taken away from her.

She couldn't feel her hands or feet. They were finally spared the agony of being ripped apart. She tried to wiggle her fingers and toes, but couldn't feel them to do it. Then she couldn't feel below her knees and elbows. Gretchen realized what was happening, but so much of her had been torn apart already, so much of who she was had become part of Amena now, that it seemed almost trivial. She could only feel her torso. Would she cease to exist? Was her consciousness going to be part of Amena? She couldn't feel her lungs, couldn't breathe. Would she still have her memories? She couldn't feel her shoulders. Would she experience things through Amena? Would she still be there, a part of the chorus of lives inside the witch? She couldn't feel her eyes. She was in darkness now. No sound either. Was this what it felt like?

She couldn't feel her

DEAD DEVIL IN THE FREEZER

By Nancy Holder

Halloween is the messiest time of year. Winds and rain splatter bright white paint and sparkling windows. Leaves change color because they're rotting; they fall because they're dead. Sad sentries, trees shiver, skeletal wrecks loyal to their posts despite the putrescence mounting around their feet. The earth stinks. Worms flourish.

Halloween is candy wrappers skittering down ashy streets and the pervasive stink of wet, sour wool. Mud, everywhere: on porches and hallways and carpets. Over-stuffed furniture picks up the odor of compost, newly turned; graveyard foulness.

Produce, forced to ripen too quickly, decomposes before it's put away. Sad, grimy sunbeams hide grease splatters and the occasional kitchen spills that, if not caught, become stains that are impossible to remove. Bathrooms never completely dry out, damp towels and floor mats mildew, and fungus attacks tile and grout.

Slippers and sweaters reek of cigarettes and old men.

~

Marie-Catherine was Mary now, a clean, precise name of four spare letters. One could be simple as a Mary, serene, untrammeled, and clean. In a family that had never ventured out of Pennsylvania, much less spoken French,

"Marie-Catherine" was a stretch onto a frontier best left to real adventurers, and after the birth of their oldest daughter, her parents went back to sensible names: Susan, Ann, and Linda.

Mary's new husband, Mark, had never known her as Marie-Catherine. Astonishingly—to outsiders—he had never met her family. Despite the fact that the two of them lived in a small town in Oregon—far from Pennsylvania—it had required some lying to prevent him from wondering about them. The uninitiated might assume that lying was complicated and messy, but it was not.

Now, as Mark came home from work, she reminded herself that she had nothing to feel guilty about. Everything she had done had been a positive step forward.

"Hi, honey," he said cheerfully, as he carefully wiped his shoes. He had left his umbrella in the stand in the mud room to dry. She knew he had hung up his raincoat beside hers, on a special hook beside the umbrella stand.

A rush of gratitude washed over her. She loved his fastidiousness, his tidiness. Mark in all ways was spare and elegant. There were no extra motions with this man; even better, no baggage—except for his single misfortune, which was to have married a woman before Mary who had neither understood nor shared his need for order. She had always been a little too busy—to put things away, to clean thoroughly, to maintain the order Mark tried so hard to create. Sometimes Mary woke up in a cold sweat, dreaming that she was still a woman like that.

Mark kissed her on the lips, once, without leaving any moisture, and smiled.

"How was your day?" she asked him.

He shrugged. "Fine. But I have to go out of town."

The words were ice water down her spine. For a moment, she was overwhelmed into silence. Then she cleared her throat and managed to say, "When?"

"I'm sorry it's such short notice." He sedately walked toward the neat stack of mail on the table. Since she had no family and had escaped all her old friendships, she rarely received anything interesting. Everyone corresponded on the net these days.

"When?" she asked again. She gripped the back of the wooden kitchen chair, holding so tightly her knuckles turned white. For a brief moment, she saw the kitchen as the wheelhouse of a doomed sailing ship, with water rushing in from broken windows and the crew shrieking for her to let them in. Then she cleared her head and looked at Mark.

"Tomorrow." He looked almost eager. "For three days."

"But it's our first Halloween together," she reminded him, trying to keep her voice from quavering.

He raised his eyebrows. "Oh. That's right. I forgot about Halloween." He tilted his chin, looking at her, perhaps seeing the panic emerging. "Were we invited somewhere?" When she shook her head, he said, "Then you can hand out the candy, all right, honey? Or just put a note on the door that says 'Sorry.' Be sure to turn off the porch light. That's what I've always done if I didn't have anything to give out."

He made it sound so simple. She closed her eyes. *You have no idea what can happen,* she wanted to say.

But she had not married Mark because she loved him. She still didn't love him. In him she had seen qualities she admired—serenity, order, self-control—and she had bound herself to him in order to model him. Like a teenager devouring a fashion magazine, so Mary was consuming Mark, but in dainty bites in case he might notice and take offense. She had no doubt that if forced to predict what Mark would do in any given situation, she would get the answer right the majority of the time. But she wouldn't be correct every single time, yet. They hadn't been married long enough.

"Is there any way you can stay here?" she asked. "It'll be our first separation."

He pointed a finger at her. "Now *that* I knew." Then he kissed her again, and laid her head on his shoulder, and said, "I'm so glad we got married."

"It was a great idea," she murmured. Then she snuggled against him and said, "Me, too. I'm glad, too."

But "glad" was as far as she was willing to go anymore. Anything stronger than "glad" could lead to trouble.

It could lead to putting things in the freezer again.

She shuddered against her husband.

"It's only for three days," he reminded her.

"Well, Christ was crucified, buried, and resurrected in three days," she retorted.

He laughed and kissed the crown of her head. "I'll be crucified if I don't go. It's a big account, Mary. If I land it, I'll be one step closer to partner."

He was a corporate accountant. She loved the concrete nature of his profession—credits and debits, career paths, steps in advancement. It was fragrant with order and lack of surprise. There was no rot in his job, or in his life.

"I'll be back before you even notice that I'm gone," he said confidently. His eyes were shiny. He was looking forward to going. She was devastated.

"You're right," she teased. But she went numb from head to toe; she was riveted with fear. She stood unmoving. He might not realize that there was a difference between economy of motion and paralysis.

"What's for dinner?" he asked.

From some heroic depths of herself, she found the ability to move on, too. "Sweet-and-sour meatballs." She made up her menus a week in advance.

"Yum."

She took this as her cue to prepare the food, although she always served dinner at the same time every night. *Or*

I usually do, she thought, seething with resentment. *Who knows what will happen now?*

Then she reminded herself that this was not a halfway house; this was the real thing. Life. Even accountants were bound to have unanticipated complications in their lives. But she was not going to receive any praise for handling the crisis. He had no idea it was a crisis.

She walked to the refrigerator and got out the ground beef. He smiled at her again and went into their bedroom. She relaxed slightly. Now he would change his clothes. He would put on jeans and a freshly laundered T-shirt and check his e-mail. It was what he did every work night. She could count on it.

She got out the frying pan and opened up the package of ground beef. Placed it into the frying pan and turned on the flame. As the meat began to cook, she forced herself not to wonder about what was in it. Ground beef was a mystery best left unexamined.

The thing about the human body was the disorder inside. Anatomy books simplified the complexities. No one had perfect little bundles of colors packed inside their chests and abdomens. Adhesions stretched and pulled across the surfaces of livers and kidneys, twisting things and attaching them to each other. Colons were loaded with polyps. Odd bits of tissues grew randomly and, like pearls in oysters, could develop into something else.

Ground beef took advantage of the disarray of cattle, grinding the entire mess into something uniform and not too odiferous. And here she was, thinking about it, when she had told herself she wouldn't.

She got a can of pineapple, brown sugar, vinegar, a green pepper. She couldn't eat onions and Mark didn't like them. He would never know that that was why she had decided to marry him. That, and the fact that of all the men she knew, he was the one most likely to help her stay in control simply because of his self-controlled nature.

She took a deep breath and opened the freezer unit of the refrigerator. No more packets of ground beef. The next container would have to come from the freezer in the basement.

The trembling began, but she managed to stop it. She could ask Mark to fetch it before he left, or simply not eat anything with ground beef in it until he got home. But what if he expected hamburgers or chili upon his return?

She could buy fresh ground beef at the store.

But what if she didn't have enough money? What if the cashier said, "Don't you have about twenty pounds of this in your freezer already?"

As the meat began to sizzle, she washed her hands. A lingering stickiness made the spaces between her thumbs and forefingers tacky; she washed them again. Then she saw the dark brown meat beneath the nail on her right forefinger and washed them again.

Mark's footfalls behind her made her jump. Her face hot, she turned off the water. Self-consciously, betraying no knowledge that he was there, she calmly dried her hands on the pristine dishtowel. She thought to herself, *When he goes back to the computer, I'll get the towel into the washing machine,* but she knew it would be better not to. He would be gone tomorrow; she could wash and scrub all day if she wanted—she'd just have to call in sick—and the day after that and the day after that.

Fresh despair surged through her. *I can't do this after all,* she thought. *It's too hard.*

Mark came up behind her and slid his arms around her waist. His nose nuzzled her behind the ear. The tightness in her throat swept across her face, freezing her smile in place. She wanted to wash her hands again before she touched him, just in case.

"Don't be sad," he said, misreading her body language,

but knowing, at least, that something was amiss.

"It's only been three months," she managed.

"It'll only be three days." He chuckled warmly, gave her a pat on her hip, and said, "I've got a couple things I want to check on the net. Looks like Campbell's Soup is going to move again." Mark had an impressive stock portfolio. He was good at predicting financial trends. Mary, of course, was not good at predicting anything. She kept her money in CDs.

The ground beef was browning. She concentrated on that. Apply enough heat, and the meat would cook. Guaranteed. Same with sexual organs, she supposed, if her husband would stay patient. They had a word for women who didn't like sex.

Mark gave her another kiss and wandered back toward their bedroom. She swallowed hard and plucked the vegetable knife from the chopping block, to cut the green pepper with.

She stared at the weapon, hard. Silvery steel. The beef made popping noises as it fried and the steel flashed. For a moment, she stood transfixed. Her knives carried a lifetime guarantee.

With a deep breath, she placed the pepper on the cutting board and expertly diced it.

Then the rain began. With a huge boom of thunder that rattled the house, it tick-tick-ticked down like scattershot across the roof. The wind tossed raindrops against the kitchen window like .22 casings. She closed her eyes for a moment. Her heartbeat was a staccato counterpoint against her ribcage. Her ears were struggling with sound; her breath was drowning stillborn in her throat.

For at least ten seconds, which is a long time, if one is counting the accumulation of minutes and hours, and then days and weeks, she stared at the bits of green pepper on the cutting board, the pleasant green muting to a waxy white against the natural grain of wood. Holding her breath, she marveled at the simplicity of the sight.

She wasn't certain, but she didn't think she had ever told Mark that when she was Marie-Catherine, she had photographed dead people for a living. If the blood had not been pounding in her ears, and she had not been spinning from lack of oxygen, she would have appreciated the irony in that phrase: making a living from taking pictures of the dead.

So many dead.

So many dead, ugly.

The meat kept cooking. She thought of other frying pans on other stoves, shoved out of the way during an argument, spilling on the floor, forgotten until the homicide was discovered; or with food rotting in houses cobbed and webbed and layered with neglect. When old people died, they weren't always missed right away. Sometimes they died very slowly—it could take years—and the precise moment between living and actual death could go unnoticed.

The brutality of murder had not gotten to her; it had been the disarray that accompanied it. The shocking realization that no matter how hard one fought the current, eventually the undertow would triumph. Chaos was the natural order, and everything wanted very much to disintegrate.

What was the use of joy if it all collapsed in on itself—all the effort and time—like the face of a twelve year-old, bludgeoned to death? Of a paw-licking cat, left with nothing else to eat?

If she could have moved or spoken at that moment, she would have rushed to Mark and confessed everything. She wasn't hiding from anyone who needed to find her. But revealing all would mean she would have to tell him that she didn't love him.

He had endured the death of his first wife, and come out whole. He still laughed, still loved, still cleaned and went to work and liked the world. From him, she would learn how to triumph over the burden.

Perhaps that would send the ghosts away.

Like the rest of the natural world, ghosts were messy.

But she couldn't move or speak. She could barely breathe. The meat was on the verge of burning: *I took so many pictures of burn victims. I have seen so much horror, I don't know how much of it really happened and how much of it has crept into my mind, like cuckoo's eggs, incubating in my mental illness.*

She watched the meat. A fine, thin line of smoke emanating from the layer closest to the edge of the pan, the layer thinnest there, and she darted her hand forward without warning. She pushed the pan just off the burner, exposing the gas flame beneath. She batted at it, too. The stinging heat seared her fingernails and she cried out, clutching her hand to her chest.

She was activated again, recharged like a robot. It was like fingers snapped in front of a hypnosis subject's face: *when I count to three, you will awaken.*

Anxiously, she glanced at the closed bedroom door.

After a while, Mark emerged, with his suitcase in his hand. He was wearing a suit, and his hair was damp from the shower. Water glistened on the strands as he came to her and kissed the side of her neck. He smelled of Irish Spring soap.

He said, "Mmm, pancakes and sausage. My favorite breakfast. You remembered."

As if by magic, the ground beef was gone; the exquisite simplicity of the green pepper against the cutting board had vanished.

The wind cackled like a witch, and Mary shivered as Mark poured himself a cup of fresh coffee. The entire scene was like something from a play; from the *Twilight Zone*. It was difficult not to dissolve into hysterics.

"Mark..." she began, unable to hide her stricken look.

"Mmm?" he asked, sipping his coffee. He sat down and glanced out the window. "I'll bet the paper's soaked." Jannela, their paper deliverer, was notorious for not putting the papers in plastic bags during inclement weather.

All she could think to say was, "Mark, it's...it's still raining. It's raining very hard."

He smiled and took another sip. "Yeah, well, I can get a copy at the airport and you can read Edward's." Edward inhabited the cubicle adjacent to hers. Mary worked for a large health insurance firm. During her initial interview, her subsequent boss, Belle Mariotte, had remarked on how knowledgeable she was about physical injuries.

The bodies she had photographed had provided her with an education akin to medical school. The condition of those bodies—ritualistically butchered or left to rot where they dropped—taught her volumes about mental injuries. The shocking thing was, most murderers were certifiably sane.

"Honey, I already told you I'd be careful, didn't I?" Tenderly, Mark kissed her cheek. "Don't forget, I was born here. I'm used to driving in weather like this."

Numb, she nodded; he must have read the anxiety in her face. She licked her lips and tried to tell him what had happened, but she didn't know what had happened. She had never lost track of time before in her life.

Grease splattered and crackled in the pan, spitting at her forearm. She didn't feel a thing. There were schizophrenics so far gone that they could burn themselves with cigarettes, and not feel it. She had taken pictures of those, too.

"Sit down," she said. "I'll serve you your breakfast." She smiled brightly. "Like your serving wench."

"Aren't you eating with me?" he asked.

"I'm not hungry." In her panic, a calm center drifted in a counterclockwise direction; if she concentrated hard enough, she could make herself stay there. Her ark of balsa wood was very nearly flimsy enough to sink there, too, but she kept saying to herself over and over, *Keep bailing. Keep bailing.*

Level sea—sea level—is here somewhere.

Her dexterity amazed her as she scooped up the pancakes and sausage. She moved like a chef; she presented like a maître d.' His eyes widened with pleasure and he picked up his cutlery. She had, apparently, set the table with her mother's heirloom silver. Somehow she had found the time—during the missing hours—to polish a place setting. *Or maybe the whole silver service.*

"Be careful," she blurted, stretching out her hand. "The knife is very sharp."

Experimentally, he pressed the blade into his sausage patty. It divided into two half-moons as easily as if they were made of butter, and not the entrails of unfortunate animals.

She had seen a gangland crime scene photo once: a man and a woman lying in pools of blood in the foyer of an apartment building. Beside the woman lay an inert Beagle. Mary had cried, "Oh, my God! They shot the dog!" For years, that had been a department joke.

Nothing else had moved her like that picture. There had been no photo crueler or more senseless. Not even the pictures of children. Those were unreal, too terrible to feel. But the dog was a concrete event, an act of violence that permeated her membranes.

The rain kept pounding. Mary thought she might scream at any moment. But that would require an explanation. If she had to tell him anything, she might tell him everything. She couldn't risk it. He was her sole tether to this world.

Or have I been cast adrift? Have I become untethered?

She said desperately, "Mark, you can't go. You just can't go."

"Aw, honey, you're so sweet." He stuffed the entire half of the sausage in his mouth and closed his eyes. "Mmm, this is so good," he groaned around the food.

~

Then he was gone, their Camry swallowed by the rain. She kept waving, in case he could see her, in case it made a difference in what happened next. Slowly, she shut the door and stood facing it for a moment, inhaling the lingering scent of spiced grease.

"That is a real thing," she whispered. "My voice is a real thing."

She could feel her feet wanting very badly to lift off the floor, sense the muscles tensing to rise up on tiptoe. She gripped the doorknob and smelled in the sausage smell, concentrating on it. It wasn't one discrete odor, but many: garlic, onion, turmeric. She inhaled other smells: the lemony tang of wax on the floor, the ever-present odor of mildew.

The house was comprised of hundreds of smells. She walked through the rooms, breathing them in as if her life depended on it, finally growing so dizzy that she had to lie down on the bed. She smelled Mark everywhere; she was ashamed of herself for constantly denying him. He was patient and kind; if her actions bewildered him, he didn't show it. Sometimes she wished he would force the issue and make her talk about her feelings. But most of the time, she was grateful that he let her be the flapping little telltale on his sail as he maneuvered into the wind.

The phone rang, terrifying her out of her wits. She reached across the bed and answered it.

"Mary? It's Edward. Happy Halloween. Aren't you coming in today?"

"Oh." She glanced at the clock. It was nine-thirty. Mark had left two hours ago. "I...I'm having some trouble," she said. "I'm not sure."

"With your car?"

"Yes," she said quickly, grateful for the lie. "It's making a funny sound. I'm not sure I should drive it in this mess."

"What kind of sound? Have you called a shop?"

"It won't turn over." She crossed her fingers.

"Sounds like your battery. Maybe something with the electrical. Are you stranded? You said Mark was going out of town."

"Oh. I...I...I'm fine."

"Listen. I'm swinging by the market at lunch. Liz doesn't think we have enough candy for tonight. I can take a look if you want."

"No, I—"

"Sorry? Hold on, Mary." He put her on hold. When he came back, he said, "I'll stop on my way to the store. See if I can give you hand."

"Don't be silly," she snapped. "It's pouring rain."

"Tell Liz that. She's convinced we'll be overrun with trick-or-treaters anyway." He chuckled. "I'll see you around noon."

He hung up. She did the same, and stared at the phone.

Then the lights went out.

Mary gave a little cry and jumped up from the bed. The room was nearly dark; the sky through the curtains was a silvery gray and there was no sun.

The living room was no better. The power was out.

The fuse box was in the basement.

It hung on the wall just above the freezer.

Thunder rolled over the roof and she wrapped her arms around herself, felt the trembling. *I can wait for Edward,* she thought. *He can go downstairs and check the circuit breakers.*

That decided, she crossed into the kitchen. The last of the coffee would soon cool.

In the shadowed room, she picked her cup off the table and carried it to the coffee maker. She lifted up the carafe and poured.

The carafe was empty.

Her face tingled; she usually made enough for a couple of cups each. She could remember drinking one cup herself, and Mark's single. There should be a lot left.

She set down the carafe as if it had bitten her.

She picked up the phone to call Edward. It didn't work.

She looked out the window at the rain. Edward's wife was silly. The kids wouldn't go out in this messy weather. All that slippery mud. Their spangles pulling off the saturated thread and net, their green and purple faces running. They would forget about Halloween.

As she listened to the rain, she looked at her kitchen, feeling as if she were seeing it for the first time in her life. She appraised it: the cracks in the grout. The shadows on the wall behind the toaster. The dishes weren't done. Sprinkles of ground coffee littered the counter next to the coffee maker.

Determined, she unwrapped a fresh sponge and got out her cleaning supplies. She sprayed cleanser, scrubbed. The rhythm of the scrubbing soothed her. *Row, row, row your boat.* She was astonished at the grime at the bottom of the sink. How had she let it get so bad?

She worked on the kitchen, and remembered triumphantly that she had meant to wash the dishtowel. Before she picked it up, she pulled on her rubber gloves. You had to be careful about germs.

The doorbell rang. *Edward,* she thought, her stomach clutching. *Go slowly. You can do this.*

When she opened the door, a shrill little voice cried out, "Trick or treat!"

She took an involuntary step backward as her next-door neighbor, Patty, laughed and caught the shoulders of JoEllen, her small daughter. JoEllen's dog, Taco Paco, went missing the week before, and the child had been very upset. But youth is resilient: the excited three-year old was dressed as a witch, in a black wig, black cape, an orange T-shirt, and an orange-and-black striped acetate skirt. She had on yellow rain boots.

"I'm sorry if we startled you," Patty said. "I saw your car in the drive and I figured you must be staying home today. We're off to Jo's preschool party." She gave her daughter a hug. "She wanted to show you her costume."

Mary tried as hard as she could to smile. Her hands began to shake. She managed, "Do you think it'll still happen? With the rain?"

"Kids and free candy? Nothing stops them," Patty said.

They looked at each other. Mary said nothing.

Patty laughed again. "Well, we'd better go. We caught you off-guard."

"No, wait," Mary blurted. "I have candy."

"We'll get plenty at school," Patty said.

"*Mo-om,*" JoEllen whined.

"It's a lovely costume," Mary said. "You look very scary. And I have chocolate bars."

"One for Mom, too?" JoEllen asked slyly.

"Yes," Mary assured her.

"So much for my diet." Patty rolled her eyes in capitulation. JoEllen beamed and turned expectantly to Mary.

"Okay." Mary swallowed hard, acutely aware of the wretched disorder of her home. "Come...come in. The place is a mess."

"You're kidding, right?" Patty asked. "My house has never been this clean."

"Mom says we're slobs," JoEllen informed Mary.

Mary turned away to fetch the miniature chocolate

bars from the cabinet.

"It's hot, don't you think?" she called to Patty.

"*Hot?* Mary, you must have a fever. It's freezing in here. It feels like it's snowing."

~

It is snowing. The officer on the scene is still there; young, chalk-white, tears in his eyes. No one is joking. When they see Marie-Catherine, they just nod.

Jake Pallamary, the coroner, is still in the bedroom with the body. When Marie-Catherine waits on the threshold, he gestures for her to come in, saying, "This is so damn sad. I guess she couldn't take it anymore."

Cancer victim. Mid-70s. Suicide.

"Sometimes death makes more sense," Jake says, looking down at the rail-thin, sunken figure dressed up in her Sunday best. "I'd do it, too, if I had cancer that bad."

He leaves the room to get something—and Marie-Catherine is alone with the body.

The woman clearly meant to do it. She obviously wanted to go.

So when her eyes open—

~

—when her eyes open

Mary's hands were filthy. There was dark brown beneath the nails. And Mary was screaming. She was screaming for all she was worth, so hot she was perspiring, and her house was a mess. The walls, the floor, the carpet, soaking and filthy, and now she was feeling, all of it: despair and remorse and guilt and rage and lust and heat and fire and brimstone; hell was the feeling of it all; hell had not frozen over, but lurked, and waited; and she had known it was waiting for the thaw. But this was fall, not even winter, this was Halloween, not December, December when the old dead woman's eyes opened and she groaned with such a depth of sorrow to find herself alive.

And she looked up at Marie-Catherine, and whispered, through chattering teeth, "Damn."

But Marie-Catherine heard what she meant: *Please.*

~

They don't find out. They never find out.

Over the weekend, they keep the old dead woman in the morgue freezer. And all Friday night, and Saturday day, and Saturday night, and Sunday day and Sunday night, Marie-Catherine worries, and goes cold and numb, cold and numb, cold and numb, so that by the conclusion of ·the autopsy on Monday afternoon, she's frozen solid. Not even the fact that she has escaped detection unthaws her.

It doesn't feel good, but she knows it's what'll save her life. So she stays frozen, a static state, which she fights at all costs to preserve. Initially she makes a few mistakes, prompting her to change her name and move as far away as possible from the scene of her mortal sin.

~

And now, here it was, all that she had tried so hard to keep in order. The disorder of what she had done, the feeling of it. The heat of it.

Her face was white hot. Her hands, burning from their task. Blisters formed along the ridges of her knuckles and the backs of her hands. As she watched, her scarlet, crackling skin blackened and began to flake off.

She was burning alive.

And the only cool place in the house was the freezer in the basement.

She shuddered and burst into tears, which were gobs

of flame that coursed down her face, carving lava tracks in her skin. Her brows and lashes ignited; the stink was awful.

Not the basement. Not the freezer.

The rain tatted, fingers tapping impatiently. In the distance, a car engine droned.

Edward.

She clutched at her burning chest and heard the sizzling of blood inside her heart. Looked down at the strange, scarlet steam.

A car door shutting.

The rain, pouring water into eddying pools of mud, graveyard sinkholes; in all the wet and cold, mold sets in. The spores are lavish and riotous; decomposition runs rampant. Chaos reigns.

Her hands had been seared down to the bones, razor sharp. In terror, she slashed her thigh with her fingertips. The sad meat was shrinking down as the fat burned crisp, and the clump plopped to the floor with a smooth cut, as if of a pathologist's scalpel.

There was knocking on the door.

Her feet were charcoal. There was no hair left on her head. The heat was unimaginable. She thought of Mark with such passion that if he had been inside her, he would have burned alive.

"Mary?"

The sound of Edward's voice decided her. She stumbled to the basement door and opened it, holding steam in her lungs as she lurched down the stairs. There were no lights, but she knew exactly where the freezer was. She had come in here whenever she felt the need to cool down, whenever the temptation to thaw rose too strongly to battle with mere willpower.

With her bone hand, she lifted up the lid and looked down at the things she had put in there. The birds, the squirrels, the occasional cat. JoEllen's missing dog, Taco Paco.

Like a pool of molten steel, she poured herself into the freezer, and with the last vestiges of solidity, pulled the lid back down. Just before it closed, she heard the front door open.

With the lid shut, Edward's screams were muffled. Softened. Cooled.

She closed her eyes. *It'll take too long,* she thought nervously.

But then she feels the arms of the old woman surrounding her, and embracing her; the dead old woman whisper, "Thank you, child, bless you," icy and soothing against her fevered temple.

Freezing again, freezing more solid.

The screams upstairs are way too hot to handle.

And way too messy.

ABOUT THE AUTHORS

Lisa Morton
Lisa Morton is a screenwriter, award-winning fiction author, and one of the world's leading authorities on Halloween. For more about her, please visit: www.lisamorton.com.

Michael Paul Gonzalez
Michael Paul Gonzalez lives and writes in Los Angeles. He is the author of *Miss Massacre's Guide to Murder and Vengeance*, *Angel Falls*, and a host of stories floating through the ether. Follow him at: MichaelPaulGonzalez.com.

Hal Bodner
Hal Bodner is the author of the bestselling gay vampire novel, *Bite Club* and the lupine sequel, *The Trouble with Hairy*. He tells people that he was born in East Philadelphia because no one knows where Cherry Hill, New Jersey is. The obstetrician who delivered him was C. Everett Koop, the future US Surgeon General who put warnings on cigarette packs. Thus, from birth, Hal was destined to become a heavy smoker. He moved to West Hollywood in the 1980s and has rarely left the city limits since. He cannot even find his way around Beverly Hills—which is the next town over. Hal has been an entertainment lawyer, a scheduler for a 976 sex telephone line, a theater reviewer and the personal assistant to a television star. For a while, he owned Heavy Petting, a pet boutique where all the movie stars shopped for their Pomeranians. Until recently, he

owned an exotic bird shop. He has never been a waiter. He lives with assorted dogs, and birds, the most notable of which is an eighty year old irritable, flesh-eating military macaw named after his icon—Tallulah. He often quips he is a slave to fur and feathers and regrets only that he isn't referring to mink and marabou. He does not have cats because he tends to sneeze on them. Having reached middle-age, he remembers Nixon. He was widowed in his early forties and can sometimes be found sunbathing at his late partner's grave while trying to avoid cemetery caretakers screaming at him to put his shirt back on.

Hal has also written a few erotic paranormal romances— which he refers to as "supernatural smut"—most notably *In Flesh and Stone* and *For Love of the Dead*. While his salacious imagination is unbounded, he much prefers his comedic roots and he is currently pecking away at a series of bitterly humorous gay super hero novels.

He married again—this time legally—to a wonderful man who is young enough not to know that Liza Minnelli is Judy Garland's daughter. As a result, Hal has recently discovered that the use of hair dye is rarely an adequate substitute for Viagra. Hal's website is: **www.wehovampire. com** and he encourages fans to send him email at Hal@ wehovampire.com. It may take him a month or so, but he generally responds to almost everyone who writes to him with the sole exception of prisoners who request free copies of his books accompanied by naked pictures.

Terry M. West
Terry M. West is a well-known author, filmmaker, actor and artist. He has written several books in the young adult field (most notably the graphic novel series, *Confessions of a Teenage Vampire*) and he has also written several

horror short stories as well as the horror/thriller novel, *Dreg*. His work has appeared (or is scheduled to appear) in *FrightNet, Scream Factory, Agony In Black, Lacunae, Jackhammer, House of Pain, Dark Muse, Moonletters, Silent Screams, When Red Snow Melts, One Hellacious Halloween, Deathmongers, Vignettes from the End of the World, Axes of Evil and Zombified 2*. He was a finalist for the 1997 International Horror Guild Award for a short story "The Night Out" and he made the 1999 Bram Stoker Award preliminary ballot for a piece of long fiction "Hair and Blood Machine." He was also mentioned on the 1997 TV Guide Sci-Fi Hot List. West's books and collections include: *A Psycho's Medley, What Price Gory?, Dead Aware:A Horror Tale Told in Screenplay, Cecil & Bubba Meet the Thang* and special collectors editions of *Car Nex, Midnight Snack* and *Cecil & Bubba Meet a Succubus*. His work has received glowing reviews. His filmography includes his debut film, *Blood for the Muse* (based on his comic book of the same name which was a finalist for the 1998 International Horror Guild Award for a comic) and *Flesh for the Beast*. He has acted in the films *The Blood Shed* and *Gallery of Fear* (both directed by Alan Rowe Kelly) and had a starring role in Joseph M. Monks' debut film, *The Bunker*. Terry currently writes and paints in Southern California with his wife, Regina, and their son, Terrence. Terry is an active member of the Horror Writer's Association.

Janet Joyce Holden
Janet Joyce Holden is a novelist and writer of dark contemporary fiction, and is the author of *Carousel* and *The Only Red Is Blood*, along with a number of short stories that appear in various anthologies. She is originally from the North of England, but now lives in Southern California. Find out more at her website: janetjoyceholden.com.

John Palisano

Fangoria writer John Palisano's short stories have appeared in *Lovecraft Ezine, Terror Tales, PS Publishing, Dark Fuse* and many more. He's also the author of the novel *Nerves*, as well as the upcoming *Dust of the Dead* from Samhain Publishing. Nominated twice for the Bram Stoker Award® for short fiction, John acts as a Trustee and is a Co-Chair of the HWA's Los Angeles Chapter. You can find him on Facebook and Twitter, or hit his site at: www.johnpalisano.com.

David Winnick

David Winnick is the author of the novel *Sulfur* and the novella "Heart of Glass". He is a blogger for Quirk Books as well as a contributing writer for *Comic Book Resources*. David currently teaches composition and literature at Chapman University where he focuses on the study of comic books and horror fiction. Once, he ate a man's soul. It tasted good, but gave him heartburn. You can follow David on Facebook, Twitter and Instagram.

Kate Jonez

Kate Jonez writes dark fantasy fiction. *Ceremony of Flies* published by DarkFuse is available in limited edition hard cover and ebook. Her Bram Stoker Award ® nominated novel *Candy House* is available at Amazon in print and ebook.

She is also chief editor at **Omnium Gatherum** a small press dedicated to publishing unique dark fantasy, weird fiction or literary dark fiction in print and ebook. Three Omnium Gatherum books have been nominated for **Shirley Jackson Awards**.

Kate is a student of all things scary and when she isn't writing she loves to collect objects for her cabinet of curiosities, research obscure and strange historical figures and photograph Southern California where she lives with a very nice man and two little dogs who are also very nice but could behave a little bit better.

R. B. Payne

Assembled from body parts stolen from the Los Angeles Coroner's dumpster, and stitched together with razor wire, R.B. Payne lives in hope of becoming human. Meanwhile, he writes.

His work can be found in anthologies such as *All American Horror of the 21st Century: The First Decade* and Permuted Press' *Times of Trouble*, and he's very proud of his analysis of three 1930's black-and-white slasher films in *Butcher Knives and Body Counts*. Upcoming work is featured in *Expiration Date* from Hades Publications and *Unspeakable Horror 2: Abominations Of Desire* from Dark Scribe Press. More information can be found at **www. rbpayne.com**.

Steven W. Booth

Steven W. Booth is an author, book designer, publisher, and entrepreneur. He has earned a BA in economics, an MBA in Nonprofit Management, and a MA in Teaching. He has been a business owner since January 2010, a publisher since August 2011, and a published author since October 2011. Steven currently owns and operates Genius Book Publishing where he publishes mostly horror and dark fiction, but has plans to begin publishing other fiction genres as well as non-fiction. His other business, Genius Book Services, provides self-publishing authors and other publishers with editing, cover art, print layout, and ebook design services. Steven is also the author of six novels. The Sheriff Penny Miller series of zombie novels (The Hungry

1 through 5), written with Harry Shannon, have paid his rent many times and regularly buys him groceries. *All the Devils*, a stand-alone thriller also written with Harry Shannon, was released in early 2014, giving Steven six published novels. Steven has been married for 14 years to a wonderful and brilliant woman, Leya. She is a math genius, and was the inspiration for the name of their companies. Steven and Leya live in Encino, CA, and are proud humans owned by a couple of cats.

Maria Alexander

Maria Alexander's stories have appeared in publications such as *Chiaroscuro Magazine, Gothic.net* and *Paradox: The Magazine of Historical and Speculative Fiction,* as well as numerous anthologies. Her debut novel, *Mr. Wicker*, was released in September 2014 by Raw Dog Screaming Press. *Publishers Weekly* calls it "...(a) splendid, bittersweet ode to the ghosts of childhood." Learn more at www.mariaalexander.net.

Eric Miller

Eric Miller works in the movie business as a screenwriter, producer, and other fun-filled, low-stress jobs. He wrote the script for *Dog Soldiers 2*, and his produced screenplays include *Mask Maker, Swamp Shark*, and *Ice Spiders*. In the book world, Miller edited the Bram Stoker Award nominated horror anthology *Hell Comes To Hollywood* and its imaginatively titled sequel *Hell Comes To Hollywood II* which also includes a story by him. His fiction regularly appears on www.HotValleyWriters.com. He lives in Los Angeles with his wife Wendy and their dog and cats. In his spare time he reads voraciously, writes occasionally, and is addicted to TV cooking shows. He is a proud member of the Horror Writers Association.

E.S. Magill

E.S. Magill is the editor of the anthologies *The Haunted Mansion Project Year One* and *Deep Cuts* (co-edited with Angel Leigh McCoy and Chris Marrs). She is also the former reviews editor and columnist for *Dark Wisdom magazine*. Her short fiction can be found in the Horror Writers Association's anthology *Blood Lite III* and *The Haunted Mansion Project Year Two*. One day she will finally finish her first novel. She has an M.A. in English, specializing in the postmodern gothic. By day, she teaches middle school English; in her spare time she dons the costume of horror writer. Southern California is home to her and her husband Greg. Friend her on Facebook and check out her blog at www.esmagill.com.

Tim Chizmar

When Tim Chizmar was a child he lost himself in evil, scary stories. One day, a morally righteous librarian refused to let him take out his books. Reading about demons, beheadings, and cannibalism wasn't the norm in Linesville, Pennsylvania. When Tim brought his mother to the library, she insisted that her son be allowed to read whatever he wanted. This upset the librarian so she looked his mother in the eye said, "Your son is going to grow up to be a great horror writer one day... or a serial killer." As of this writing, Tim hasn't killed anyone. He has, however, written and sold many short stories and screenplays. When he's not burying bodies, Tim is a director, comedian and producer living in Los Angeles, CA. What drives Tim's success is knowing that somewhere in Pennsylvania a librarian is praying for his soul.

Robin Wyatt Dunn

Robin Wyatt Dunn was born in Wyoming during the Carter Administration. He lives in Los Angeles.

P.S. Gifford

PS Gifford was born and raised in Birmingham, England but has called California home since the 1980s. Over the last dozen years his short stories, essays and poems have appeared in dozens of magazines and have been included in several anthologies. He also has four collections of his twisted short stories available at all good on-line book sellers. He is currently working on his first full-fledged novel with his trusted canine, Sir Winston, perpetually at his side. For more details please visit www.psgifford.co.uk.

Xach Fromson

Xach Fromson is one of the creators and hosts for the Los Angeles based reading series Shades & Shadows. He is a native Angeleno, with a lifelong passion for horror, science fiction and dark fantasy. He has a BA in Creative Writing from California State University Northridge, and an MFA in Creative Writing from UC Riverside Palm Desert.

Nancy Holder

Nancy Holder is a New York Times bestselling author and recipient of five Bram Stoker Awards. She writes novels and episode guides for "universes" such as *Buffy the Vampire Slayer, Teen Wolf, Hellboy, Beauty and the Beast*, and others. She also writes and edits comic books and pulp fiction for Moonstone Books. She would like to send a shout out to Ian R. Faulkner and *Cemetery Dance* for helping her retrieve this story from the freezer. She lives in San Diego.
Twitter:@nancyholder Facebook: https://www.facebook.com/nancyholderfans Website: www.nancyholder.com

All contributors are members of the HWA (Horror Writers Association) Los Angeles chapter. To find out more about the national organization visit http://horror.org.

www.ingramcontent.com/pod-product-compliance
Lightning Source LLC
Chambersburg PA
CBHW060210180626
46813CB00007B/2777